BY WINSTON GRAHAM

CORDELIA

NIGHT WITHOUT STARS

THE RENEGADE

DEMELZA

FORTUNE IS A WOMAN

VENTURE ONCE MORE

THE LAST GAMBLE

THE LITTLE WALLS

THE SLEEPING PARTNER

GREEK FIRE

THE TUMBLED HOUSE

MARNIE

THE GROVE OF EAGLES

AFTER THE ACT

TAKE MY LIFE

THE WALKING STICK

NIGHT JOURNEY

NIGHT JOURNEY

NIGHT JOURNEY

WINSTON GRAHAM

1968

DOUBLEDAY & COMPANY, INC., GARDEN CITY, NEW YORK

*All of the characters in this book
are fictitious, and any resemblance
to actual persons, living or dead,
is purely coincidental*

Night Journey was written in 1940 and published in 1941. It sold about 700 copies and then the type and sheets were destroyed in an air raid.

It is one of only two spy stories I have ever written. Since its day much has happened to the spy story and much to the spy. Life in the sub-world of espionage has become more savage, more sophisticated and more ambivalent. Yet I hope this novel may still perhaps have some small interest and some entertainment value—both for itself alone and because it was written in the darkest days of the war. I have revised it for this publication, but have not attempted to alter its judgments with the superior hindsight of twenty-five years.

W.G.

NIGHT JOURNEY

CHAPTER 1

It was a shock when my sister came to tell me that the police had called. She was upset by it too; but then for the last few years the police of any country had had that effect on Nina. It wasn't pleasant to see that anxious furtive look on her face again. I resented the fact that she should have to feel anxious even here.

I took off my gloves, threw them on the slab, followed her into the living room.

Sergeant Evans, whom I know of old. I thought he looked in some way more official than when he had last called about two weeks ago. Not good, that.

"Well, Sergeant," I said rather pettishly. "Quite a familiar visitor, eh? What this time? More regulations? Sit down. You can drink a cup of coffee?"

"Thank you, no, sir." He stood by the window, feet firmly apart, taking authority from his native ground. The sun, falling obliquely, threw across the room a shadow of him that was not a precise silhouette. "I'm sorry to say that they want you at the police station again."

I looked at my watch. "Well, it's inconvenient. I'm working, you know. Could I call round this evening?"

"Well, I'm afraid not, sir. I was told that they wanted to see you right away, sir. And to bring a small suitcase with a few personal belongings."

Outside, the starlings were twittering.

"Robert," Nina said, "they're going to—"

"Does this mean—"

"I honestly don't know, sir." Sergeant Evans looked out at the dahlias to disclaim responsibility. "Maybe it'll only be for tonight. Anyway, there it is, I'm afraid."

It was impossible to understand what this new development could mean. Surely they could not intend to reverse their previous decision—and so soon.

"Whose instructions?" I said angrily.

"I don't know, Dr. Mencken. Someone up above somewhere. That's all I can tell you."

I shrugged, and then tried not to shrug, feeling that the overexpressive gesture was not English.

"There's nothing more to be said, then, is there? Give me five minutes to put a few things together. Make coffee for the sergeant, Nina."

But instead she followed me into the barn that I had laboriously converted into a laboratory.

"Robert, let me come with you this time. It may help in some way. And besides, I want to be there!"

"It wouldn't be any use at all, *mein lieber*. Anyway, they would not let you come. Don't worry. I shall be home tomorrow. Think it out for yourself! What point would there be in releasing me only a month ago and now interning me afresh?"

"I'm not so sure," Nina said. "You can never be sure what

12

people will do in wartime—even people who have never been invaded for 900 years."

I turned out the gas-jet and took the tubes from the retort. "Precautions have to be taken. After what happened in Norway and other countries in May, can you wonder that everyone is on edge? This is another routine inquiry. I'll be home to lunch tomorrow."

But in fact I was not so confident as I sounded; not at all sure of myself as I sat beside Sergeant Evans in his two-seater coupé and drove with him that bright early September afternoon of 1940 to the police station two miles away in Reading. All that Nina said was true: you could not depend on even reasonable people in wartime. Officialdom and red tape are always needlessly unfeeling because they interpret a set of rules according to the book and not in terms of the individual. There were many instances of this in my previous internment.

I am glad no one saw me enter the police station for I am still sensitive about these things. It is perhaps a middle-European attitude of mind. Ten minutes in a bare little room with war regulations posted on the wall, and then Sergeant Evans said that Inspector Donnington would see me.

A bald, rosy-cheeked man was behind the desk in the inner office. I had not met him before.

"Sit down, Dr. Mencken, I'll not keep you waiting a minute." He went on writing until a constable came in with a file holding together some official buff-colored forms, four photographs and two handwritten reports. When we were alone again he studied these. I felt very uneasy. Once you have been tried and found guilty, even if it is only the guilt of being the wrong nationality, the sensation sticks.

Inspector Donnington was now studying one of the photographs and comparing it with the original sitting opposite him. I tried to look as if this was no business of mine.

"I'll just run over the main facts of your case, Dr. Mencken, to see if we have them accurately. I'm sorry to have had to bring you in again."

"*Gar nicht*," I said under my breath.

"Your name is Robert Gustav Mencken?"

"Yes."

"You are an Austrian subject, born at St. Pölten, near Vienna, of an Austrian father and an English mother. You are thirty-one years old and a doctor of chemistry. This is an Austrian degree?"

"That one is, yes. The University of Vienna."

"You also, I understand, have British degrees?"

"I was made a doctor of science at London University last year. And I am a Fellow of the Institute of Chemists."

"You first came to England in June, two years ago?"

"I came here to settle then. I had been over on holidays before. Three vacations."

"You are unmarried and have no relatives except your sister with whom you live. Is that correct?"

"I have no very near relatives, true. My mother died last year. But her brother—my uncle—lives in Leeds. My father died in 1938 and a few of his relatives are in Vienna still."

"Your father was in Austria when he died?"

"Yes, in a concentration camp."

Inspector Donnington looked up and coughed. He turned the paper over. "Was he of Jewish blood?"

"No. It was his misfortune to have served as Minister of the Interior in one of the early Social Democrat Governments."

"I see . . . You have no more reason to love Hitler than we have, then. I understand that."

"Thank you," I said stiffly.

"To return to your own case, Dr. Mencken, I see from these reports that you were able to leave Austria in June 1938

14

with the help of the Society of Friends. You lived in London for a year and then rented the house where you now live. On the outbreak of war you—er—came before a tribunal under the chairmanship of Mr. O'Casey and were granted a "C" certificate exempting you from the restrictions applying to enemy aliens. In May of this year . . . I don't quite follow clearly what happened in May of this year."

"After Holland and places, after what happened there, the Government set up Regional Advisory Committees to re-examine all the cases. But you will know that, naturally. I beg your pardon. Well, I was summoned before them and re-examined and again given a 'C' certificate. But only a week after that, when the fifth columnist scare was at its height, I was arrested without notice and sent to Prisoners of War Internment Camp No. 3. I was there two weeks before being drafted up to Liverpool to be sent overseas. But by then the Council of Austrians in Great Britain had appealed on my behalf and I was returned to Worcester."

"Yes, I understand that. And then in early August it was finally decided to release you again because you were doing work of national importance, eh?"

I listened to the drone of Hurricanes overhead.

"Since then," I said, "I have thought all my troubles were over, but this seems to have been an optimistic view."

Donnington hunched his shoulders until his neck disappeared. "Well, it's like this, Doctor. The Home Office, as you may know, has taken over the camps and the question of aliens in general; but when it comes to the pinch the War Office still has the last say. And I don't mind telling you that at the moment it must have. News has come through that we are to expect an invasion any day—almost certainly within the next ten. So the military have issued orders for the temporary re-internment of any aliens who have been set at large. I'm sorry to have to do this, but those are my orders."

I felt frozen, unable to think it out.

"May I be allowed to write to my sister this time?"

"Oh, yes, you'll find a big improvement in conditions generally in the camps. Last time it was emergency measures for everyone. And I don't—and if nothing too bad happens, I don't suppose they'll keep you much after the end of September. It's got to come—the invasion, if it comes at all this year—has got to come within the next three weeks." Inspector Donnington rose.

"And my work?" I said, in exasperation. "It has already been delayed by months, and I assure you it's not useless."

He shook his head. "I'm afraid it'll have to wait for your release, sir. We can't very well provide you with a laboratory in the camp, can we? But if it's papers you want—if it's anything you can do in the camp—I'll be very happy to pass on instructions to your sister. We'll see that anything she sends will reach you."

"I'm obliged." I stared at the bright shafts of sunlight on the papers on his desk. They even lit up my photograph, the one taken by the Viennese security police, in April 1938. "I question if they will really risk the invasion while you—while we—still have some control of the air."

"That we don't know. You will have seen that the best predictions date it for the day after tomorrow."

"In that case," I said, "I should be more use with a rifle—if you have one to spare—than locked away in an internment camp."

He looked at me narrowly.

"I daresay you would. But I'm afraid this is a case where ninety-nine innocent people have to suffer because of the odd black sheep who may be among them."

CHAPTER 2

So much has happened since then that it is quite hard to remember just what those early days were like. The danger of invasion was acute; later it became chronic and therefore in a sense a commonplace. So memories are overlaid and one tends to forget the apprehension and *qui vive* of a whole nation.

Yet for me as a part-alien, even as a part-pacifist, there had been a curious exhilaration in the thought. One might die. But one might live gloriously. Whatever happened there would be no more shame. So I took my first internment with great bitterness. It seemed like a sudden stab in the back—the uttermost insult.

Of course I should say at once that physical conditions had not been too bad even in May. They were Utopian compared with the treatment we should have received in the countries of our various origins. It was the psychological shock that hurt, the incredible moral insult of being herded with men of pro-Nazi and pro-Fascist sympathies. In the matter of a few hours there were arguments, quarrels, open fights among us: factions and cliques, bitter enmities grew overnight. An old Italian journalist who occupied the bunk next to mine said one day:

"Patience, my boy, that is what is needed for us all now. We of our type who have suffered and striven for what I suppose we can, without a sneer, still call democracy . . . who have become penniless and lonely and outcast . . . who have come to live in one of the very few lands—the last in Europe, almost—which still stand for the things we hold . . . We feel betrayed because the people here seem, in the final crisis, to have turned against us. . . . But patience, it was bound to happen after all the other betrayals. A little time and we shall be free again."

I grew very much to admire old Gentile Farino. Unfortunately his freedom came earlier than it should have done, for he was transported to Canada on the *Arandora Star*, and when she was torpedoed he went down with her.

But this time . . . this time I had no cause at all to complain of being herded with Nazi sympathizers. I had no cause to complain of being herded with anyone, because I was kept only one night in Worcester and then was transferred to a quiet place near Hereford where the buildings were hardly finished and the number housed was so few we could have had a hut each to ourselves. All the same I fretted and fumed at the waste of time, the boredom, the inability of officialdom to see into my brain and discover that it held no ambition more passionately than the defeat of the dictators. I prayed for rain with the ardor of a farmer in a drought, because it was obvious that the danger of invasion had to be considered imminent while the weather held. But each day was as bright as the last. My sister wrote that she had again appealed to the Council of Austrians and was determined to make a public fuss even if they did not. I wrote back to tell her to do nothing of the sort, since the probable reaction of a government already overburdened with work would be to intern her as well.

Six days went, and then I was called out one morning and conducted by a sentry to a fine old Queen Anne house I had glimpsed before, set among beeches and not yet quite surrounded by Nissen huts. The house was empty, but in an anteroom off the paneled hall another interviewer was waiting.

Star and crown of a lieutenant colonel; a slender, blue-eyed soldier with a limp and hair thinning and graying. Air of authority so tactfully concealed that you imagined he hardly ever had to exercise it. I knew his type, the introspective man of action that the British Army—and the Austrian Army—sometimes throws up. The direct opposite of the Blimp, and rarer, but just as much a product of the same society.

"Good morning. Do sit down, Dr. Mencken. Whisky and soda?"

"Thank you." Somewhat surprised at this. "But weak please. I seldom drink."

"That's all to the good, isn't it," he said, obscurely. "Lovely house this; maybe you've seen over it?"

"No."

"Did you notice the overmantel in the hall? Grinling Gibbons or his school. Must have been brought here, as the house isn't old enough."

"I will look as I go out."

"Good to be able to live in a place like this. Doubt if anyone will be able to afford to after the war."

"So long as there is an 'after.'"

"Yes. Yes." He handed me a glass and now limped over to an armchair opposite me. "I expect you're feeling sore about your re-internment, aren't you?"

I smiled bleakly. "Not happy, shall we say."

"That's diplomatic anyway. . . . You know, the military have had to stand up to quite a few brick-bats over this internment question, Dr. Mencken. Questions in Parliament concerning the limitations of the military mind and what happens when the War Office is in full cry. Oh, there's some truth in it, I won't deny. But I'd like you to know that the wholesale internment which took place in May was only finally decided on in the interests of the aliens themselves."

"Oh," I said.

"It's an old story, that the refugee alien is not always a free agent. From 1935 to 1938 hundreds of men and women were granted permission to leave Germany and enter France and then told privately before they left that their permits were not in order. They were then kept in touch with the Fatherland under constant threat of being exposed and forced to return." The colonel sipped his whisky. "And any number of refugees of unimpeachable character and long records of oppression in their own country have betrayed the country that accepted them because of fear for their relatives. If you do not obey the commands of the Führer your mother or your brother or your sister or your wife will disappear into Auschwitz. Many cases have come to our notice in the last few months alone."

"I see that. But I think you must know that I have no near relative in Austria whom I need fear for."

"Certainly we do—and did. But to intern one alien to protect him so that he cannot obey the Nazis is not usually quite sufficient. Enough people must be interned with him so that no suspicion arises that he has told the truth to the authorities. Otherwise the threatened relative may suffer all the worse."

"It's obliging of you to explain this. I see the difficulties . . ."

"But this does not explain your arrest last week?"

"I should like to think it did."

He laughed. "You're a younger man than I expected to meet, Dr. Mencken."

"I'm thirty-one. You must know that."

"I do. I mean in manner. For your academic distinction, thirty-one is in any case very young."

"It somewhat depends how you start. Most people spend seven years as children on general subjects; a liberal education they call it. I started very early on what interested me. Therefore I know quite a bit on some subjects—on others virtually nothing at all."

He leaned back in his big leather chair—so slim that another could have sat beside him. "Would it surprise you to know that of the seventy-three thousand three hundred Germans and Austrians in this country, you are the only one who was re-arrested last week?"

I shifted uneasily. All this friendliness and lack of ceremony. . . . What action of mine recently could possibly have been misinterpreted? That letter I wrote to Gilligan at the Royal Society? My demands to the electricians for extra power points? My telephone call to Leeds?

He was watching me closely. "This work you are doing. It's of national importance, I understand."

"Among other things, I am working on a process for utilizing sisal waste in submarines."

"Would you say that is of vital national importance?"

"I don't quite understand. All such processes are of exceptional value in wartime. This not more so than many others. Not less so either."

"Would you consider yourself indispensable to the country's effort—say for a couple of months? I understand there are other men working on the same idea. Professor Martin, for instance, of Edinburgh."

"You know him? Then you must know as much about all this as I do."

"You think Professor Martin is likely to succeed independently of you?"

"I have not seen him since May. He's a clever man and has better facilities."

"More whisky, Dr. Mencken?"

"Thank you; I've not finished this yet."

He looked out of the window, his blue eyes unfocused as if temporarily he was thinking of something else. "Would it be true to say you were an expert on the subject of poison gas?"

I thought this out. The alien problem, sisal waste, and now gas. Even for a chat over after-dinner port it seemed a little disconnected. "No. I would not call myself anything like an expert."

"But you gave a course of three lectures on various gases at London University the first winter you were here."

"Those," I said, "were ionized gases."

He paused. "I didn't know. I thought . . ."

"I'm sorry."

There was nothing absent-minded about his eyes now. Someone was going to get into big trouble for that mistake.

"Those lectures," I said. "In any case they were not very profound. I was invited to give them because I had been a friend and confidant of Kaufmann in Vienna. I was reporting some of the original ideas of a great man. There was little original of my own in them. And anyway—as you will know— that is really a branch of atomic physics."

He had risen and gone to his desk, picked up a paper and read through it. "But I understand from this that you did some work on poison gases when you were in Vienna."

"Ah, yes, a little, when I was younger. But when I was twenty-six I gave all that up."

"Why?"

"By then many of us in Austria could see the writing on the wall. As an Austrian, Hitler would never be content without possessing Austria. If he did take it I knew I would not want to stay. (Always, of course, I have been half English in sentiment.) But if my work there was such that it could contribute to military knowledge I knew I should not be allowed to leave. So I turned to other things."

"Very farsighted of you." He was still staring at the paper.

"You see," I said, "in spite of having avoided a liberal education I am really rather a jack of all trades. It is not really the way to achieve eminence."

"Suppose," he said, "you were to see a gas manufactured in a laboratory, and demonstrated; would you to able to tell in what way it differed from a known gas, and—and recognize and remember the elements going to its composition?"

"Oh, yes. If I had full access to the laboratory."

He nodded. "Perhaps it's time we stopped beating about the bush, Dr. Mencken."

I said I thought it was.

"You have been very patient. But in a letter to your sister—I'm so sorry but these things are always intercepted— in a letter to your sister written last Saturday you complain rather bitterly of this country's lack of confidence in your patriotism. I think we can prove to you now that we have a very real confidence in your patriotism—if you'll allow us to make use of it."

"I hope I can."

"Well . . . it's no sinecure that we offer."

Outside, some machine was at work. I think it was a reaper, cutting and gathering the mixed corn that grew on the one-time lawn in front of the house.

"My name is Brown," he said. "I belong to the Special Branch of the British Intelligence Department. A little while ago we had word from the head of our northern Italian organization, appealing for extra help for a job which had come their way and asking if we could supply it. This we have been considering. The help they need is only one man. But unless that man conforms to certain definite requirements he would be better not sent."

I sipped my whisky. Now I needed it. "I conform to these requirements?"

He smiled suddenly. "That, for the last two weeks, we have been trying to decide. The requirements are that he must be completely trustworthy, and able to keep his mouth shut if things go right—or still more if they go wrong. He must speak Italian like a native and know German too. And he *must* be a first-class chemist. That is the great difficulty."

"With some knowledge on the subject of poison gases?"

"As you say."

"Anything else?" I asked with a touch of sarcasm.

"He must be prepared to face all that such a mission would entail. Since we are at war, I imagine that goes without saying."

I felt rather unwell. Half an hour ago I had been an interned alien with no immediate prospect of release and with only one prospect before me if I *were* released: a return to the seclusion of a laboratory. Now a sudden new world was open. I felt like a bird suddenly freed and too suddenly confronted with the menaces which were a part of freedom—there was already a yearning for the protection of the cage.

Adventure and danger were well enough for those who were used to it. I was not. Very far from it. I had always had too much imagination, and too much solitude in which to exercise it, to be a brave man. This thing I was being offered might need courage of a high order. Better to refuse

1

now than to fail miserably later and involve others in the failure.

"What physical qualifications?" I asked.

"None."

"There's no question of my having to—to impersonate someone else?" As soon as I asked I was ashamed of the question.

"Nothing like that. We might perhaps have preferred someone a little older, but . . ."

A vitally important and unpleasant factor was that I knew myself still to be an Austrian citizen. If I were discovered in Italy and not shot out of hand I would be sent at once back to Germany. In the back of my mind hung the menace of the concentration camp and the *tötschlager*. Even after two years in England I could still wake up in the night sweating. And we had only been under direct Nazi rule for four months before we left. It is well to be brave. It is very enviable to be brave . . .

"Have you anyone else in view?"

"Not anyone nearly so suitable."

"What assistance would I have?"

"All that could be given you. You'd make contact with some of our agents over there and they would have everything arranged. With luck you could be back in England for Christmas."

Agents. Cardboard figures. Notes pushed under doors and hidden in bouquets of flowers. Passwords, secret signs, seedy men standing in shadowy doorways scattering cigarette ash. Cardboard figures who would become real.

"I still don't understand what you would expect. What would I have to do?"

"Attend a conference of Italian and German scientists in Milan on October the fourteenth and fifteenth."

I got up and walked across to the window, peered out. It

was a reaper. I wiped the palms of my hands with a handkerchief. In a very nasty way indeed I was caught with my own grievance. As Colonel Brown had said, my complaint all along had been that England was mistreating her adopted sons by putting them behind barbed wire. The least she could do was give them a rifle and let them fight. I'd said as much to Inspector Donnington. Well, now I had the opportunity I had been demanding. But it was neither what I wanted nor what I had expected. I would have given two years of my life to get out of this piece of war work that was being offered me. But the challenge was flung down. And in a sense it was a private challenge. How would I live with myself if I refused?

"Very sorry to take so long."

"Oh, no, it's better to see all round it first. Sleep on it if you wish. But I must know tomorrow."

"What about my sister?"

"I'm afraid you wouldn't be allowed to communicate with her. If we could have done this more openly we should not have gone to the trouble of arresting you."

"I see. I see. So, so far as the outside world is concerned, I should remain interned."

"Yes. Of course you can write to your sister. You can write a number of letters to her which can be dated ahead and posted during the next month. You can also write another letter—if you feel you'd like to—which would be sent to her if your mission fails. We can arrange all these things very easily. The main thing is the decision. But do take your time. Because, once this thing has been undertaken, there can't very well be any turning back. I may say," Colonel Brown smiled, "I must say, that there's no question of blackmail on our part. If you refuse you'll be released before the weekend."

"Thank you. I appreciate that." I finished the whisky, wishing now for a stronger refill but not liking to ask. "Colonel Brown, if I take this, if I do this, I would like to strike a bargain. . . . Just before the war I applied for naturalization papers. These had not come through when war broke out, and since then they have been refused. Well, I am tired of being neither one thing nor the other. If I take this on I wish an undertaking that there will be no more difficulty."

"There will be no more difficulty, Dr. Mencken. I can promise you that. In fact—"

"In fact?"

"I must tell you that these papers will come through in any case."

"Very well," I said, feeling very sick, "I'll take the offer. Now please give me more details."

But first, and in a friendly way, he gave me his hand.

CHAPTER 3

Great adventures seldom start ostentatiously, and the second stage of this one began even more quietly than the first. There was in fact, I suppose, a certain proper drama in my arrest, the sharp severing of an ordinary life, my laboratory left untidy, a letter half written, a meal in preparation, a book open face down on the bedside table. But the second stage had only secrecy to commend it.

I left Liverpool in a little tramp steamer, one unit of a miscellaneous and ragged convoy bound for Lisbon. No one even came to the quayside to wish me luck. I walked up the gangway with a single suitcase, hat brim turned down and collar pulled up against the thick Merseyside drizzle. I thought of that distinguished English lady who had been in the Bahamas at the time of Dunkirk and had immediately left to return to her own country to see how she could help at such a time of danger and catastrophe. To the first person she met in England—the officer examining her passport—she had

exclaimed: "Isn't it dreadful! Isn't it dreadful!" And the
officer had looked up and said: "What? What? Oh . . . yes,
it's been raining like this for three days."

The thought and what it implied was a comfort to me
now. I wished I had more of that spirit myself. I felt I
might need to remember its message in the days ahead.

Shaded blue lights on the quay, the throb of engines; crew
all too busy to pay me attention, but one detached himself to
show me my cabin. I had hardly unpacked my few things
before the little tramp was under way. I had already seen the
last of England, for when I went on deck half an hour later
the land had vanished into mist and darkness.

For some days the weather had shown signs of breaking,
and we met autumnal winds. I am a miserable sailor, and the
long trek round the north coast of Ireland was an experience
which only Biscay forced me to forget.

Not a pleasant trip, but between bouts of nausea I reread
Bergendorff's *Der Chemische Krieg*, and Meyer's *Der Gas-
kampf und die Chemischen Kampstoffe* and several others.
I felt myself out of date and out of touch.

The Tagus safely, and not an enemy plane or ship; but
once or twice I had been so low that a periscope would have
been a diversion. Lisbon as the only neutral Atlantic port was
a clearing house of gossip, and I found it crowded with
refugees washed up like flotsam by the tide of Nazi aggression.
All nationalities and political colors rubbed shoulders in the
common misfortune: French socialists and Polish aristocrats,
Belgian cabinet ministers and Rumanian oil magnates, Dutch
bankers and Spanish republicans. Germans too, men of importance in the National Socialist world. One I recognized
whom I had last seen in the third car of Hitler's triumphal
entry into Vienna. Perhaps they wished to be sure that
Portugal should not feel neglected.

Feeling better with dry land underfoot, I went at once to

seek out the man who had been told to expect me. I located him in the maze of narrow streets below the National Library and near that pleasant shady square, the Praca. A Jew and a seller of antiques, he was so much like Gielgud's Shylock that I expected him at any moment to cry, "An oath, an oath, I have an oath in heaven: Shall I lay perjury upon my soul? No, not for Venice."

In the event it would not have been inappropriate.

But in fact he was not concerned for my soul nor for his own, but only for my personality. I lost it. In the back room of his little shop, I lost it, together with luggage, books, clothing and Anglo-Austrian identity. No change in actual appearance, but I found that my name was now Edmondo Catania, that my passport had been issued by the Italian government, that I lived in Lisbon and occupied a comfortable flat overlooking the gardens of St. Pedro de Alcantara and had an office in the city from which I carried on a business as agent representing one of the largest silk exporters in Rome. My hair, said my passport, echoing my old one, was dark brown, my eyes gray, my height five feet ten inches. I had been born in Turin and my age was thirty-five. I was, it seemed, returning to my own country to volunteer for military service.

This patriotic plan I now put into practice, traveling over-land to Madrid and thence to Barcelona. From here I caught another tramp steamer bound for Venice, and spent the early days of the voyage reading some papers which had been provided and which I was respectfully requested to commit to memory and then burn.

Colonel Brown had really told me very little of what was ahead, and these papers were nothing to do with the future. They only told me what sort of a man Edmondo Catania had been in the past.

Even though this little tramp was a neutral, the captain

seemed in no mind to take undue risks, with the sudden collapse of France, and trigger-happy Italian and British warships liable to appear over the horizon at any time, so we hugged the coastline most of the way, and as a result we did not reach Venice until the afternoon of October the ninth, when she berthed four days behind her own pessimistic schedule.

I was very anxious now. Four important days had been lost and might ruin the whole enterprise for lack of time. No one had said where I must stay, so I booked a room in a hotel overlooking the Lagoon and unpacked my few things. Nothing now till nightfall.

Strange to be in this loveliest of all cities again after five years, especially so after the dangerous and depressing journey, first across wide and devious stretches of sea in a state of unsleeping armed alert, then across country still showing the blight of civil war—that civil war which had been a symptom of the ailment of which all Europe was now sick. The last time I was in Venice the Spanish sore hadn't even begun to fester; and Schuschnigg at least was still alive and a free Austrian cabinet still met—whether it was to consider the Fatherland Front or the future of comic opera; and the shadow of a bloodstained neurotic despot had fallen across my beloved Vienna, but only the shadow. That Europe in which I had grown up had never been a real place. In it men had worked and played and tended their own affairs, not quite conscious, but never entirely unconscious, of the insecure, fluid, temporary nature of it all. Like ants building in ground soon to be returned.

The differences which war had brought to this city of pleasure seemed at first quite few. Many of the gondola men still plied, but the water buses were happily fewer; the enchanted St. Mark's Square was scarcely less crowded for the time of year, the pigeons as numerous and as well fed. Shops were still stacked with beautiful silks, tooled leathers, costume jewelry, Murano glass, shirts, embroidered blouses, rich materials, *haute couture* fashions. The grocery shops and fish shops were full, fruit shops were overflowing. I had forgotten that I had now been moved to the winning side.

Perhaps the greatest difference was in the languages. I heard no English, no French, only once American, twice Spanish. Being a polyglot, I am sensitive to the dialects of others; and I could pick out Bavarian from Prussian, Saxon from Westphalian, northern Italian from Roman; twice with something of a thrill I heard pure Viennese.

Only when dusk fell did more changes show. The brilliance of the cafés and the lights round the Piazza San Marco had gone, as had all the lights except navigation lights on the lagoon. Even the lanterns in the gondolas had been dimmed; they moved through the narrow canals like glowworms, and the gondoliers called their peculiar cry more often at corners so that they should not bump into their fellows. The great clock of the Campanile was not lit. The Lido was invisible. The cathedral and churches were not floodlit. All this seemed to me a great improvement.

The day had been bright and clear, but toward evening a watery mist crept over the sun, and now in the dusk a feeling of damp crept over the city. Depressed, I went back to the hotel.

The depression was perhaps more one of instinct and foreboding, because so far everything had gone without a hitch. The first big test had come on landing from the ship and passing the port authorities, but the questions asked had been well within the scope of a man who knew Edmondo Catania as well as I did. Of course the secret police had been hanging about, and one of them had listened to my answers, but I had been used to them in Italy for a long time, and they seemed no different from before the war. Mussolini's Mafia, my father had called them, because the Duce had truncated and rendered innocuous that earliest of racketeering organizations by the expedient of incorporating its leading members in his secret police.

So I had signed at the hotel and filled up the various forms with a first creeping sense of confidence. One hears frequently of the liar who tells his story so often that he begins to believe it himself.

After dinner out again. In the semidarkness of St. Mark's Square the murmur of voices was like the movement of the sea. As I walked across it one of the café orchestras began to play *Sibella*. Venice, like a popular woman surrounded by her suitors, was anxious that sterner preoccupations should not lure them away.

At the Café Florian I ordered coffee, but the waiter said coffee was not obtainable and brought a substitute. I sipped it, and it was not good, so I drank the ice-cold Dolomite water that came with it. War, I thought, was exposed as the ludicrous thing it was when it enforced rationing and blackout curtains in the square where Tintoretto and Titian had walked—or, equally, I suppose, gas masks at a Buckingham Palace levée.

But not this war. There could never really be anything ludicrous about this war, however it manifested itself.

The mori swing back their hammers to strike nine o'clock on the Torre dell' Orologio, and then the great mellow bell of the Campanile took up the note, to be followed by all the other clocks of the city having their moment's chatter before silence was imposed again.

I got up. Time to go.

I left the square by the Piazzetta, but after crossing the Rio di Palazzo turned sharply into the town by way of a narrow street lined with wine shops. Here the Venetians and the less well-off come to sit and drink and gossip in the narrow alleys and behind darkened windows filled with gaudy bottles and *fiascos* of chianti. In a few minutes I came to a square empty and quiet. I crossed it and the humped bridge beyond, where dark green viscous water lapped bits of refuse against the edges of the steps.

As always Venice was quiet away from the hubbub of the Piazza. An occasional figure passed me, boots clattering on the stone flags. A cat, angular and nervous, stared at me from a doorway. Another with feline, fastidious grace sniffed an empty tin. Two children, pale and bony-legged, marched past whistling *Sibella*.

I had had no reason on earlier visits to seek out the Campiello di Giovanni, but I had bought a map in the hotel, and in another three minutes I stood at the corner of the square. It was flanked with tall old houses and with a café on the corner, from which came the amplified music of a radio. The square was stone-flagged right across, and in the center was an old stone wellhead from which the inhabitants had once drawn their water supply.

Dim light came through the blinds of the café, but I passed it and made a slow circuit. An old crone whispered at me from a doorway. Five lire changed hands and her complaints died away. In an upper room of a house nearby someone was playing a piano.

I went to the center and sat on the stone wall of the well. The sky was clearing again, and the night breeze as it came in from the sea had a chill in it. Grotesque statues, moon silhouetted, peered over the roofs from a church near by. The pianist lived on the opposite side from the café, about four stories up.

He was playing *Tales from the Vienna Woods*. A couple of sailors walking across the square took up the refrain and could be heard whistling it as they disappeared down a narrow alley. He played quite well—some foreigner, probably come to Vienna on slender means to study and to enlarge his spiritual horizon. So one would have thought.

A piece by Handel or Bach was begun, but half way it faltered as if inspiration was lacking, changed to Chopin. One of the waltzes. A Flat Major, was it?

I walked over toward the corner to hear it better. It was third floor after all, not fourth. The window was open and chinks of light could be seen as the breeze stirred the curtain.

A door without number or name. Turn and go in. A small dingy hall: the low-powered electric bulb shielded with brown paper showed doors, a telephone, a pot fern, stairs. I went up them.

On the second floor a door was open and light striped the worn linoleum of the landing. A child in a white muslin nightdress was sitting in the open door trying to mend a doll. I did not offer help, though she looked as if she expected it. Four doors on the third floor, but light under only one. I tapped.

Chopin went on. Exuberant trills and octaves were leading up to the finale. I tapped more loudly.

The music stopped.

"Chi cosa dite?" a voice called.

I went in.

CHAPTER 4

A big untidy room that looked as if a jackdaw had been collecting newspapers. Wicker chairs and Turkish rugs, lace curtains behind blackout curtains; a baby grand and a fat man with a stump of a cheroot between his irregular discolored teeth.

He had started on the music again and I waited until the piece was over, standing self-consciously in the open doorway.

"That was very fine," I said in Italian. "You must play it for me again sometime."

He got up and shut the window, then walked over and shut the door behind me.

"I'm damned if I do. They might have chosen something less hackneyed. You're four days late, Signor Catania."

We stared at each other.

"Mussolini's navy was not able to issue a navicert," I replied.

I had of course known that the pianist would be no long-haired, fine-featured student; but the reality really was rather a disappointment. A man in the middle forties, of medium height, with small self-confident black eyes, a sallow skin that would never stay shaven long enough to look clean. A smart but greasy blue suit with pin stripe, big blue and white spotted tie and spotted handkerchief to match, too much of it showing. He looked like a man with a deficiency of ascorbic acid, one who took too little exercise and ate too many sweets. A prosperous bookmaker or the manager of a high-class brothel. But his fat was not soft fat.

"Sit down," he said in English, speaking with an intonation I couldn't place. "Name of Andrews. So you're Mencken."

"Edmondo Catania," I said. "Would you wish to see my passport?"

"Thanks, no. I know more about you than you do yourself. When did you get here?"

"Two o'clock this afternoon."

"Any difficulties on landing?"

"No. They seemed to approve of my coming home to enlist."

His cigar wagged and he showed more teeth. "We were getting that anxious, wondering what had happened to you. It's been left pretty late now. You must meet Captain Bonini first thing in the morning."

On the threshold of the task I suddenly found resolution failing again. Courage had come with me like a noisy crowd to a town gate: now, faced with the guards, it was melting away.

"Bonini?"

"Yes. Sit down and I'll tell you about him. Cigar?"

I took one—not that I wanted one—sat down. His face was close to mine as he offered me a light. Garlic and cheap scent. His eyes were dogmatic but his cleft chin weak.

He said: "You are half British, aren't you?"

"Yes."

"What's the other half—German?"

"Austrian." He must have known.

"Much the same thing, isn't it?"

"Not to me."

"Hitler's a Bavarian. You're part of the *Herrenvolk*."

"I am not ashamed of my Austrian blood."

"Ah, well, no." He sat back and crossed his fat legs. "It takes all sorts to make a nation. I must confess I don't exactly adore Germans. It's a weakness, you know, a weakness in an agent to have likes and dislikes of his own."

"I wouldn't think that. It might be a mistake to have prejudices."

He blew out a cloud of smoke. "I've got those too."

Silence fell. I noticed a ladies' fashion magazine open among all the newspapers, some French novels; calendars on the walls advertising Chianti and Valpolicella.

"Bonini," I prompted.

"By the way, don't call me Andrews. My name is Brevio. Michele Brevio. You feeling a bit het-up about all this?"

"I left England knowing practically nothing," I said, annoyed.

"All this cloak and dagger stuff. It must be unsettling, oh, I agree. But in fact most of it's dreary routine. I hope yours will be. Try to look on it as that."

I waited while he screwed out the last half inch of his cigar.

"Next week, this conference in Milan. It's something quite separate from political discussions like meetings on the Brenner Pass and powwows between Keitel and Badoglio. Chief man at this meeting is Professor Brayda. Heard of him?"

"No."

"About six weeks ago we got news that he was on the track

39

of a new poison gas. He's going to demonstrate it. Then another scientist has an electromagnetic improvement for aerial torpedoes. We've already got most particulars of that. A top German scientist will be there, representing his government and following the general policy of pooling information."

"And you expect me to attend? How can I?"

"Wait. I'm not sure of the number of people who'll be at this conference, but apart from the half dozen scientists and their assistants, there'll be officials representing the services. The Admiralty will send a Captain Bonini who's attached to the Scientific Division of the Naval Staff in Venice. You will go as his secretary."

So that was it. It would have been kinder for Colonel Brown to have told me. But perhaps Colonel Brown did not know.

"You are lucky," I said, "to have found a traitor so highly placed. Is he trustworthy?"

"Neither a traitor nor trustworthy by choice. Fortunately he has one hobby—beautiful women, and one preoccupation— himself. It's a good combination, Mencken. I've been playing him, through an intermediary, for a couple of years. Perhaps it would reassure you if I told you about that first."

"As you please." Andrews had this slight accent but I could not place it. The inflexions of the various English counties still sometimes puzzle me.

". . . he loves some woman and she has expensive tastes; so he must gratify them. But not only pretty girls can be exacting: so can creditors, so can the social demands of his position; he has risen quickly in the navy by his own scientific talents but he has no family, no money behind him. So he goes to a credit house recommended by a friend of mine, run by a friend of mine. He is given a loan on good security. He repays part of this but later borrows more—on less good security. He also repays part of this. But why worry?" Andrews spread his plump pale hands. "Why worry? The rate of interest is low. The head of the credit house is tolerant and has become a personal friend. There is no hurry to repay. So the loan gradually increases.

"But eventually, quite suddenly, the source of the bounty dries up. The credit house would be glad of a substantial repayment. Captain Bonini cannot oblige. He is irritated. The house should know his position by now and also his expectations. The money is perfectly secure against his future salary. One cannot produce money out of a hat. So good. The matter is dropped. But three months later it is raised again. The credit house itself is to some extent embarrassed and must have some repayment. Bonini cannot make it. Dear, dear, this is very unfortunate. If he were to be bankrupted it would ruin his career. But stay; an idea. The head of the credit house has a brother who is head of a foreign news agency in Venice. The agency has asked his brother for particulars of the new Italian destroyer which has just been launched. Naturally he cannot get them. But if Captain Bonini were to get them they would share the payment when it was received."

Andrews took out another cigar and clipped the end. "Captain Bonini does not like this idea at all: it savors of treachery, and Bonini is a patriot. But eventually after careful consideration he agrees. When the information is obtained he is pleasantly surprised at the amount paid him—and also secretly amused. For although details of the destroyer are not yet released to the Italian press he happens to know that they are familiar to every Naval Attaché in the country, no attempt having been made to keep them secret. Otherwise he would in no circumstances have consented to obtain them. But naturally he does not tell his friend this. Am I boring you, Dr. Mencken?"

41

"Not at all."

"Well, you see, this goes on. From time to time now he yields to the temptation to earn easy money, and if now and then he refuses to do something because he thinks the release of the information is prejudicial to Italy—then no pressure is brought to bear on him. So everyone is satisfied. Captain Bonini keeps his conscience clear and his pocket not too empty. From time to time it has no doubt occurred to him that the information asked for is outside the scope of the ordinary news agency, but he thinks it better on all grounds not to inquire too closely. A nice balance, as you'll appreciate. However, when Italy enters the war this is all changed. He calls a halt. It is the end. He is a patriot. No more information, however innocuous. His conscience won't allow it."

A puffing and blowing at the cigar.

"For the first time my friend, the head of the credit house, shows his teeth. What of the money still owing, he asks? It will be found. When? In good time. Sometime will not do; it must be found at once. How? The usual way. No, no, it is impossible. Nothing is impossible except to back out now. Captain Bonini makes his last stand. Very well, he will go down for his principles. Let them bankrupt him for debt; he strikes an attitude; sooner that than betray his country. (Perhaps he thinks he is calling their bluff.) But suddenly they no longer threaten bankruptcy; that is nothing. If he backs out now, information will reach the Fascist headquarters in Rome that *for over a year he has been selling information to a foreign and now an enemy power*. Corroborative evidence, painstakingly accumulated, will accompany the disclosure. It is not now his pocket or his pretty ladies, no, indeed, nor even his career which are threatened, it is his life. Mussolini has a short way with traitors. Captain Bonini blusters and threatens, but eventually gives in." An expressive gesture with two bent thumbs. "The fish is landed. He can struggle no more."

Andrews took out his bright spotted handkerchief and wiped his neck. The room was warm and the story had been told with energy.

"An unwilling traitor is always dangerous," I said.

"All traitors are dangerous, Mencken, whatever their personal feelings. But that is how we live. That is how we have to live. I'll give you his address and full instructions before you go. As his secretary you should be accepted without question. Once you've made contact with him you'll be under his orders until you return to Venice. But I don't think you need fear that Bonini will let you down, because on your safety depends his own."

The smoke he had given me was really a cheroot and was strong and green. It tasted as if the leaves had been plucked about a week ago, and most of the time I let it burn like a dangerous fuse between my fingers.

"How do I make contact with you again?"

"Come tomorrow afternoon at six. Then not again until it is all over. You'll be in Milan, I expect, about five days. And that Veronese product, Valpolicella, is in my opinion superior, *signore*, to most Bordeaux wines. Naturally it is a matter of taste, but given perfect conditions . . ."

He had changed not only the subject but the language. His hearing must have been very acute, because someone then knocked on the door.

"Come in," said Andrews. "What do you drink in Lisbon, *signore?* Not only Port, I hope. I find the flavor too heavy for my palate . . ."

A tall thin man came in. He leaned against the side of the door warily and looked at me with faded blue, bloodshot eyes. Then he closed the door and coughed.

"Hullo," said Andrews. "Hullo, Dwight."

The thin man inspected the room with his eyes as if he thought it was going to jump out at him.

"Is this—"

"Yes, it's Mencken. Here at last. I wondered if you'd come round."

"Well, thank God he's come. About time. Any trouble?"

"None at all," said Andrews, for me.

"Thank God for that. So the gallop's going through as arranged?"

Andrews seemed to remember that I was not one of his wine calendars. "This is Major Berczik, Doctor. A colleague of ours."

I got up uncertainly, put down the smelly cheroot, shook hands. Just bones gripped mine. A *very* thin man with cropped iron-gray hair and tight skin shiny and brown from the Italian sun. His long narrow face with its strong cheek bones had an equine look. I thought he sized me up as if I were the unexpected winner of a Selling Plate.

"Younger than I thought," he said in English. "Much younger. Maybe that's no matter. Mustn't look a gift horse in the mouth, eh, Andrews?" His thin lips parted in an unsatisfactory smile. "See anything of the British Navy? Damned good job they didn't sink your old tub."

"I've been explaining the position to Dr. Mencken," said Andrews softly. "He will meet Captain Bonini tomorrow morning. Smoke?"

"Not one of your damned poisonous weeds. Smell like something out of the Sargasso Sea." He continued to assess me. "You have my sympathy, old man. Hope you'll finish the course. Big things may depend."

"I'm a beginner at this work," I said despondently. "Don't expect too much." I felt their attitude was too lighthearted and casual and, indeed, callous. It was not how I understood conspiracy.

"The British Intelligence," said Andrews, "always expects too much. That's how it gets results. Major Dwight has arrived from Rome on this job, by the way. He'll be in Milan during the conference and you'll be able to get in touch with him if things go wrong."

The other man noticed the expression on my face. "That's me, y'know. Dwight by birth; Berczik by adoption. Major in either event. Dragoon Guards, to be truthful." He was filling his pipe, a worn old briar, but stopped and coughed, a loose rustling cough. "I've news for you, Andrews. The name of the German scientist who's attending the conference. Dr. von Riehl."

"Von Riehl," said Andrews. "He's been in Italy a fortnight already. Have you heard of him, Mencken?"

"Yes," I said slowly. "But I question where the 'von' has come from. He was Professor of Chemistry at Bonn five or six years ago. Since—"

"Did you ever meet him?" Dwight asked sharply.

"No, no. But I know he was promoted by the Nazi government to be one of their top scientific advisers. I did hear that he was among the chief advocates of biological and chemical warfare."

Dwight smiled, if you can call it a smile when only skin and not flesh is involved. "A worthy representative of the Reich. He'll get the Iron Cross, no doubt."

For some minutes they discussed the ways of Germans with bitterness and acidity. I wondered if they had ever heard of Goethe or Beethoven, Freud or Schweitzer or Einstein. I had a curious presentiment that Andrews would never like me, because of my Austrian blood. I am not a man given over to quick antipathies, and this feeling surprised me.

"What's the man been doing in Italy for over two weeks?" Andrews said. "He brings a Fräulein to Garda, apparently for what people do go away with Fräuleins for, and then almost every day drives off with his secretaries: to Milan, to Turin, to Genoa, leaving the girl behind."

Dwight said: "Von Riehl is conferring with the various industrial and economic boys; he's been sent to get what information he can and report to his government on the exact condition of Italian war production, especially its most urgent needs in raw materials and ersatz products."

"Ah . . . that makes sense."

Dwight made a wet noise in his pipe and looked at me over the top of it. "Things are shortly going to move in Africa, Dr. Mencken. Italy has to act more vigorously than she has done so far, to justify her rating as a major partner. All Germany expects it. But war wastage will be high and Italy is cut off from her normal markets. Also things are not well with either her war machine or her supply system. Von Riehl has been sent to find out what's wrong. Next Tuesday, near the end of his stay, he's attending this conference of scientists under Professor Brayda. From what you say, it sounds as if that's really more his line of country than reporting on inefficiency and bottlenecks, but maybe he's a man of all-round ability."

"He's that," I said. "He is the breed of scientist who is much better at organizing a department than doing original research. Where is the conference to be held?"

"At the big experimental laboratories attached to the Faroni works."

"Oh, I know where that is."

"What sort of a memory have you?" Andrews asked.

"Poor for most things. But good on my own subjects, I suppose."

"You see, you'll have to play this as it comes. You may be allowed to take a few notes—I don't see why not—but it'll depend a lot on how well Bonini supports you. You'll be there after all as his secretary. Have you ever done any photography?"

"Afraid not."

"Pity. We've a nice little job that looks just like a gold wristwatch. You pull your cuff back to see the time and *click*. . . ."

"No," said Dwight. "That would be a non-starter in inexpert hands—and dam' dangerous. Let's be content with Dr. Mencken's report. We don't want him to fall at the first jump."

He began to cough again, and got up to change his position. He coughed till the veins stood out on his narrow shiny forehead. Pulmonary edema, most probably.

"Blast," he said. "Where was I? Oh, the camera—"

"Chlorine or phosgene?" I asked.

He stared at me. "Phosgene," he said after a moment. "Thiépval, 1916. I'd forgotten you were a doctor chappie."

"Not really. But I had a cousin in Vienna. He had got it fighting on the other side. . . ."

Andrews waved this irritably aside. "Do you know where the Fondamenta Vittoria is, Mencken?"

"Not for certain. In this area?"

"Near the Arsenal. You'll find Captain Bonini at number five. Be there at eleven tomorrow. He'll be expecting you. Give in your name but don't state your business until he comes. Report back here about six tomorrow. In the meantime I'll have your passport. I'll get it visaed for entry into Switzerland."

I put out the end of my cheroot. "You expect me to return that way?"

Andrews took my passport and stared at it. "Not *expect* We'd like you to return the way you came. But Switzerland is the nearest neutral if anything goes wrong."

47

Walking back to the hotel, I thought that I did not find either of my helpers congenial men. If only one of them had been like Colonel Brown. But charm is not an essential for a secret agent; ruthlessness may be. In neither of these men, I thought, would scruples be a serious handicap.

All the same I wished they had been more secretive, more serious about it all. They might have been talking a trade; they seemed casual, careless. I hoped this was a misconception, that they would be careful with their own lives and specially careful with mine.

CHAPTER 5

The Fondamenta Vittoria is, as its name suggests, a row of houses overlooking a canal. Its view must have been very pleasant on a sunny morning, but today there was heavy rain. I had come by gondola to save getting wet and the gondolier, having demanded four times the proper fare and received only double, made a play of complaint and annoyance. The servant who came to the door let me in and closed it again to shut out his guttural tenor.

Yes, Captain Bonini was in. What name? Would I be pleased to wait? She showed me into a handsome hall with a baroque marble staircase worthy of Longhena. I stood admiring this, and then turned nervously at the sound of slippered footsteps, to see approaching a man almost as handsome in his own way as the staircase. The noble beauty of the young Italian is sometimes enough to take the breath away. This man was ten years beyond his best and was now putting on weight; in another five the flowering would be

49

over; but he still impressed, with his glossy hair, pale olive skin, magnificent eyes. Of course none of this was any guide to his character: the Borgias probably looked the same.

"Captain Bonini?"

"You asked for me."

"I was admiring the carving of the balustrade, sir. It is distinguished."

"Early eighteenth century. After the style of the Trinita dei Monti. What do you want?"

So it seemed that he wished to hear my prepared story. "I approach you with diffidence, sir. We are related through my cousin Edda, who married your brother-in-law. I have lately come from Portugal where I was in the silk trade. I was to have joined the forces but yesterday I was rejected on medical grounds. It occurred to me that in your capacity on the naval staff you might—might hear of some clerical work that I could do."

He felt in the pocket of his brightly striped silk dressing gown and fitted a cigarette into a long white holder. He did not offer me one. I wondered why the interview was in this public place and it occurred to me that he wanted to try to cover himself in case of trouble. If he could bring witnesses to this first meeting . . .

"*What* relation are you to Edda? She has never mentioned you."

"Her mother and mine are sisters. Her mother married a Rosselino and mine a Catania. My family still lives in the Via Montevecchio, Turin, where I was born."

He lit the cigarette. "We have no room for the unfit in Italy. You had better have stayed in Portugal."

So he was to have his little unpleasantness.

"I wanted to help," I said humbly.

"No doubt, no doubt. . . . What can you do?"

"I can type and write shorthand. I can speak German.

Also a little French. I have had some training in office methods."

"So have many others. I'll keep your case in mind, Catania, but I can promise very little. Where are you staying?"

"At the Hotel San Moisé."

"Very well. You will excuse me. I am busy now; I have important matters to attend to." He walked to the bell and pushed it. Throughout the interview he had hardly looked at me; his manner was detached, cold; if it had been more personally involved it would have been hostile.

The maid appeared. "Show this gentleman out."

"Thank you," I said, "I shall hope to hear from you."

"Don't rely on it. Take something else if you can get it."

The interview was at an end. It did not seem quite to have turned out as arranged, but I was in his hands.

As I got to the door he said: "Stay," and came padding across with his vigorous, slightly flat-footed walk. "Did you say you could speak German?"

"Yes, sir, I know it well."

"To be able to interpret for me if necessary?"

"Oh, yes, certainly."

"Oh, then I might be able to offer you a temporary post. I wonder. My own secretary has been taken ill and may be off two or three weeks. I have important business to attend to in Milan and need someone I can trust. I will put the matter before the Admiralty and see if I am permitted to use you temporarily."

I tried to change from hang-dog to eager dog. "That is most kind. Thank you. I shall look forward to working for you, sir."

He stood with the holder firm between his strong white teeth. "We would have to get a security clearance. I don't know if it would be possible in the time, but come and see me tomorrow morning at eleven. I shall know then. But don't build on it. The decision will be out of my hands."

The maid was holding the door open. "Thank you. I'm greatly indebted. Most obliged."

He didn't reply but turned away in a whisk of bright silk dressing gown as I went out into the rain.

Venice is not an unfriendly city even in bad weather; and I bought an inexpensive umbrella and spent the rest of the morning in company with many other umbrellas shopgazing in the Merceria. I had lunch at a trattoria and then spent a pleasant half hour in St. Mark's Cathedral—though nothing inside it can compare with the old painted Byzantine beauty of the exterior. I walked back to my hotel wondering what had happened to Bonini's own secretary. How did one conveniently arrange for someone to be ill, if that someone were not in the secret?

In the afternoon the rain stopped and I went for another walk, fed the pigeons and at five-fifteen found myself in the Campiello di Giovanni.

Andrews had said about six, but this seemed near enough for an inexact appointment, so I climbed the dingy stairs, threading between three children playing on a lower flight, tapped on Andrews' door. There was no answer. He would be out.

I tapped a second time just to be sure, and instantly the door was open and Andrews stood there.

He bulked. He took most of the light somehow. There was not much room for anybody in the doorway but him. I resisted—and slightly resented—an inclination to step back.

"Well?"

"You told me to call round this afternoon."

"Not at this time."

"About six."

"It's not yet nearly six."

"I'm sorry," I said stiffly. "I will come back."

"Hell, no. Come in. It won't do to be up and down the stairs all day."

He moved aside and I went in, swallowing offense. I was clearly in the wrong. "I'm sorry. Next time you want me at six don't say 'about' six."

He picked at his teeth. "There'd better not *be* a next time. What have you to report?"

I told him.

"Good. What do you think of the animal?"

"Bonini? Handsome but dangerous. I don't trust him. He might any time try to save himself by turning King's Evidence."

"Duce's Evidence, you mean. He would if he could. But all espionage is based on probabilities; certainties don't exist. How do I know that you are not a German Nazi at heart? How do you know that I am not paid by the Italians as well as by the British?"

I stared at him, half angry, half doubtful. He seemed to enjoy taunting me; yet logically my brain acknowledged that he was right.

"I think if you'll give me my instructions—"

The door on the left of the room opened and a young woman in a dressing gown came in.

"What I'm surprised about—" she began in English, and then saw me. She looked at Andrews. Clearly I was adding to her surprise.

Andrews picked something out of his discolored bottom teeth with a fingernail. "Come in, my dear. This is Robert Mencken, recently from Portugal; you've heard me speak of him. This is Jane Howard, an Australian with American connections."

She came in, buttoning a couple more buttons of this

peach silk flowered housecoat. Underneath I could see she
wore only a black brassière and short black knickers.

She half smiled and murmured a greeting, and I made some
stiff conventional reply, understanding very well now why my
too early call had been so unwelcome.

She was a very attractive girl.

In my life I have had little time for courting women or
making love to them; but I have always enjoyed women's
company and they seem to have enjoyed mine. Perhaps it has
helped that there has been a lack of challenge in my attitude,
but never a lack of interest. Just at the moment of course I
was off balance, concerned only to make an excuse which
would end this embarrassment and enable me to leave; but
I still could not help but notice how very attractive she was,
and wonder what she could possibly see in Andrews.

We made a few moments more of conversation, but I was
guarded, aware that Andrews obviously confided too much in
his mistress. What *was* the point of introducing me as
Mencken when it should be Catania?

"My passport," I said to him, refusing a cigarette, "I should
be glad to have it now."

"Of course. I'll get it." He scratched his plump chin. "But
there are one or two things I still have to explain to you."
He went off into the room from which she had emerged.

The girl lit the cigarette she had just been given. Her quiet,
serious face bent over the lighter, dark curling fringe over
pale brow, lashes hiding brown eyes. This done, she perched
on the arm of the only easy chair in the room, one slim leg
swinging free, the mule an inch or so fallen away from the
heel above it. She had brought a scent of jasmine into a room
not previously oversavory.

"Had you any problem with Captain Bonini?" she asked.

So she knew the whole story. Where in God's name did
Andrews' confidences begin and end? The man was impos-

sible. Colonel Brown had delivered me over to a lunatic who risked not only my freedom but his own.

"None so far. D'you know him, Miss Howard? . . . Or perhaps I shouldn't call you Miss Howard?"

She smiled again. "Perhaps you shouldn't. It's Mrs. Howard, to be correct."

"Oh . . . I'm afraid I had not thought of that. My memory was being overtaxed with Bercziks and Brevios."

"A lot of Bs, aren't there," she agreed. "Berczik, Brevio, Bonini, . . . I've seen Captain Bonini more than once. The last time I saw him—at a social function—he tried to get me into a private room."

"I don't wonder," I said.

Her eyes widened slightly, but before she could reply Andrews came back.

"Here it is. All set for the next stage."

"Is this visa genuine?"

"No, Mencken, it isn't. But no frontier official will be able to tell the difference."

Mrs. Howard slipped off her chair arm and tapped the cigarette in an ash tray. "Excuse me." She went back into the bedroom.

Andrews and I ran through our little lesson. "That seems to be all," he said. "Now before you go, is there anything else you want? The less we meet henceforward the better."

"I'd like to know how many other people have details of this scheme."

His small black eyes went over me. In any account of me there wouldn't be a detail missing.

"You don't need to worry about Jane. She's as tight as the Bank of England. She has to know because she's helping in this."

"D'you mean she's a part of the organization? I thought—"

"Yes, indeed," said Andrews, as the girl came back. "One

55

thinks a lot of things. But anything you like to ask is all right with me." He scratched the balding patch on the crown of his head and then carefully smoothed back the thin black hair with his fingers, patting it over and over again. "Going, Jane? Let's see, had I a job for you?"

She had taken off her dressing gown and replaced it with a frock, a neat black thing of wool or something, with padded shoulders which made her look younger and still more slim.

"About the radio?"

"That's it. What I felt was—"

"It's time I went," I said harshly. "There's nothing more to arrange, is there?"

Andrews took his fingers from his head and looked at them. They were greasy. "Nothing, except to remind you to put the minimum on paper. Nothing if you can avoid it. Say things over in your head until you're sure of them. So—good luck, Signor Catania."

He had the politeness to wipe his fingers down the side of his jacket before he shook hands.

She must have followed me from the square quite soon and by chance have taken the same route; she overtook me in the Calle San Zaccaria as I stopped to look in a window.

I would have let her pass, but she stopped and spoke. There seemed no reticence in any of them.

"Yes," I answered, "I'm staying at the San Moisé."

"I know it," she said. "It's got that cute little landing stage where the gondolas can moor."

We walked the length of the street together, through the Sottoportico and out on the Riva degli Schiavoni. This was its usual scene of bustling activity. Postcard stalls, scarf stalls, cameo stalls, strolling crowds, cameras clicking, gondolas bobbing and milling in the churned up waters of the lagoon, a naval pinnace leaving an anchored destroyer; three fishermen, unshaven for a week, mending their nets beside a gaunt and shabby fishing boat; a low-built cargo ship, flying the swastika, in tow of a tug; the smell and feel of the sea.

"I love it here," she said, but in Italian now. "Have you ever spent a whole winter here? They have a fair on this quay. Roundabouts and things and candy stalls."

"I have never been in winter," I said. "We used to come for holidays when I lived in Vienna. But it's almost five years now." I took a breath. "It's strange. Little in this city has changed; but Europe has become a madhouse since then."

"Perhaps," she said, "you ought to forget that you ever knew Vienna. It's much easier to live a part if you live it all the time."

"I have not been encouraged to do that since I came."

We stopped at the foot of an equestrian statue and she bent to light a cigarette. Her hair wafted about her face, making little magic moves over cheeks and eyes. "Vernon is naughty about these things. It's a—sort of outlet. He has many responsibilities."

Natural that she should defend him. "Where do you live?" I asked. "Or is that not permitted?"

"Yes, yes. On the Grand Canal. With my husband." She straightened up, eyes glinting in the light from the sea.

"This is out of your way, then."

"No. I can get a vaporetto from San Zaccaria."

"How is it you can stay here so openly?"

"My husband is American so I can claim his nationality."

This privilege was clearly one she did not repay with fidelity. It was all rather difficult, for she did not give me the impression of being a young woman with alley-cat morals. Perhaps my mind was too conventional. Human types cannot be classified as if they exist in a laboratory.

All this, somehow, did not make her any less interesting. But then perhaps from the first sight my attention had been riveted. The subtle chemistry of attraction is something that this chemist does not even ask to understand.

I walked with her to the landing stage and then, having seen her off, strolled across St. Mark's Square toward my hotel. It was a pity, or it seemed to me a pity, that I should probably never see her again.

CHAPTER 6

Captain Bonini next morning at eleven. The grim business of deception.

He kept me waiting half an hour and then came in naval uniform. The smart severity of the uniform took away from the fleshiness of his figure; I think he wore a body belt.

We met in a small anteroom and he at once came to the point. "I have been given limited permission to use you for as long as my own secretary is away. This will not be long. Please let me see your papers."

"I am extremely obliged to you, sir. You are very kind to have taken this trouble."

He waved an irritable hand—a hand strangely like Andrews' at first glance, soft and plump and flexible, but lacking some implication of a *dangerous* softness.

"My family," I said, "will look on this—"

"Save your breath," he said. "Understand if I engage you, you are here not to talk but to obey orders."

I was dutifully silent while he thumbed through the papers. "That seems satisfactory," he said at length, grudgingly.

I picked them up from the marble-topped table on which he had dropped them as if they were dirty.

"There is nothing today," he said, "and tomorrow is Sunday when I shall be off duty. Call here at eight-thirty on Monday. On Monday afternoon, you will go to Milan, to the Hotel Colleoni, where you will find two rooms booked in my name. I will join you on Tuesday morning. I shall want you to attend a conference with me on Tuesday afternoon. This will last for two or three days."

"Very well, sir."

"Do you understand anything of Naval Ordnance?"

"Er—no, sir. But I did reach a good standard in mathematics and physics."

He grunted. "I have some papers here for you to study. Make what you can of them. It is not necessary to understand them fully but only to grasp some of the terms. You may spend the morning in this room. When you have done put them in this drawer. Do not be late on Monday. Is that clear?"

"Yes, sir. And thank you."

He left me, clearly intent on doing his part with the minimum of politeness. In some degree perhaps this helped him to salve his uneasy conscience and his fear of being contaminated.

The papers he had left me were the sort he must have pulled out of some odd cubbyhole to lend an air of reality to the charade. They dealt with subjects like armature windings, the permeability of high quality steel, theories of magnetic reluctance. They could well have had bearing on one or other of the subjects at the conference but were of an elementary nature. I carefully read through them, and could not resist adding a footnote to one paper where the writer was making deductions from an incomplete knowledge of his subject. That done, I walked back to the hotel for lunch.

The weather was overcast again today and the lagoon had none of its familiar color. Andrews had said it would be more discreet for me to stay in the general vicinity of the hotel; but the public rooms felt too public and my bedroom was far too private. Although all arrangements were going according to plan, my imagination would not let them alone. Pitfalls, it seemed to me, yawned everywhere. How had Bonini so easily secured clearance for me to attend a high-power scientific conference, an unknown relative engaged arbitrarily as his secretary? Were security arrangements sufficiently lax in Italy? Even if *he* thought he could get me in, I might well be turned back at the doors. Even if I were admitted, as a secretary I should not be invited to examine things as a scientist would, and I might miss the points most needed. If I tried to discover more I would only draw attention to myself. I was no practiced spy. At school I had always been the one to be found out.

So, against Andrews' advice, I went for a long walk. I took a vaporetto to the Rialto Bridge and then wandered on north through the Strada Nuova among the Venetian shops and courtyards. Past San Giovanni Crisostomo, I strolled through tiny slits of streets and over narrow bridges. I thought of what Venice must have been like before the introduction of the humped bridge had abolished the horse and made the gondola the universal means of transport. I eventually found myself at the extremity of the island at the church of Madonna dell 'Orto, and then, not wanting to go farther on toward the station, had to retrace my steps to the only bridge, near the Ca d'Oro, which led back into the eastern part of the city. I ate an ice cream opposite the Church of

Saints Giovanni and Paolo and admired Colleoni's magnificent statue. Then home, feeling footsore but more relaxed.

At the hotel they told me someone had been ringing me on the telephone. No longer relaxed, I dined early, hoping for the best and speculating on all the different varieties of trouble this could mean.

The Gorgonzola had been reached when the waiter came across with the half-expected message. Three kiosks at the door of the hotel. One had the receiver off its hook.

"*Pronto,*" I said.

"Signor Catania?" A woman's voice.

"Speaking."

"At eight this evening there will be a gondolier at the steps at the side entrance of your hotel. He will wear a white kerchief. If you engage him he will bring you here." Click.

"Who is that speaking?"

No answer.

"Who is there? Are you there?"

The line was dead.

I came slowly out of the kiosk. Foolish to ask unnecessary questions. Only yesterday I had listened to her guttural pronunciation and reflected that she had it both ways: an attractive colonial burr in English, this soft broken accent in Italian.

I went back to my dinner and finished it quietly.

"Signor Catania?" said the gondolier. He was a tall youngish man with the hooked nose of a true Venetian and a mop of fair hair. He had only one eye, which may have explained way he was not in the armed forces but gave him a sinister look. I thought of a voice carefully imitated, a gondola ride by night, a blow on the head, a splash in the bottle-green water . . .

"You are from . . . ?"

"If you will be seated, *signore*."

I looked around. The commissionaire from the hotel was listening. I got in the gondola.

It rocked gently as we were pushed away. I leaned back in the cushions and curtains of the closed interior. It smelled dusty, and of some spicy scent like sandalwood or pine. There was a crude blue picture of the Virgin and two post-cards of lesser saints. We moved off, not toward the Grand Canal but away from it.

The night was very heavy, with ribs of cloud almost blotting out the moon. My gondolier seemed to be taking a tortuous route; certainly I soon lost direction. At times we slipped silently between the tall bare houses, the only sound the ripple of water and the plash of his oar, the only light the shaded lamp on the *ferro* of the gondola. Now and then we would run beside a narrow alley, and a half blacked-out street lamp would cast the shadow of the gondola behind us, until it crept up, monstrous and misshappen, overtook us and stretched ahead, to merge into a waste of darkness. At times we slipped underneath lines of washing hung across the canals, and there were cats everywhere, mangy, emaciated, half wild, slinking in the shadows of a gutter or peering with savage eyes from the elevation of a wall. Life had never been easy for the innumerable cats of Venice; it would be much harder as the people felt the scarcity of war.

I put my head out. "Is this some roundabout route? How much longer shall we be?"

Some light reflected from his splendid teeth in the darkness. "*Si, signore,* I understand your haste."

He understood more than I did, but I could not argue. I sat back and waited. We had already been moving half an hour.

The water ahead abruptly widened and I saw that at last we had come out on the Grand Canal. We crossed hastily to avoid one of the steamboats which bore down on us hooting dismally in the semidarkness.

A narrow canal on the other side. Slippery walls, slime-grown piles, a smell of darkness and decay. The tide was low. We were drawing up at a narrow landing stage with mooring poles and a tall green-painted door. The gondolier helped me out and smilingly accepted a twenty lire tip. I stood and watched him pole away cheerfully into the darkness before I turned and pulled at the bell.

CHAPTER 7

She opened the door herself, and at once.

"Please come in. I'm real sorry for this mystery. Mind, there are two steps."

We went up narrow carpeted stairs into a neat little modern dining room; then we crossed a passage and she pushed open a wrought-iron gate into a larger room with a finely molded ceiling and long velvet curtains over Moorish windows. The furnishing was modern Italian work, chosen to match a few pieces that were plainly antique and valuable.

So the lady was wealthy too. Her affair with Andrews had no grosser side. She was wearing a pale primrose-colored frock, tight and rather long. I watched her cross the room with that characteristic, fastidious walk I had already come to recognize. She walked like a cat picking its way among leaves.

As she pulled the curtain to cut out a nick of light, I said: "Does that look out on the Grand Canal?"

"Yes. I told the gondolier to come round the back way."

"That was not the only back way he took. It was all in the best traditions of melodrama."

"This work is often true to its traditions, Dr. Mencken."

"I suppose so."

She looked at me from under her lashes. "I don't even know if I've done right to ask you here, but Major Dwight is already in Milan and Vernon Andrews has gone to Verona. I thought this the best thing to do—safer than saying anything over the telephone."

"Something has gone wrong?"

"I'm not sure, but I felt I had to warn you. All today you have been followed."

Worm twist in stomach, twist like falling from a height, like a dagger's turn, like a sentence of death.

Try to be casual. "I wonder what that means."

She sat on the edge of a chair and picked up a silver embossed cigarette box, offered me one. We lit up. It was an unfortunate moment for my hand to hold a match to her cigarette.

"Captain Bonini might wish to keep an eye on you over the weekend, for his own personal reasons," she said. "Or the police may keep a general surveillance on people newly arrived from abroad. Anything is possible. But it means you mustn't have any more contact with us—not merely for our sakes but for your own."

"You'll let Andrews know?"

"Of course. It might mean some change of arrangements after the conference."

"If I reach the conference."

To my regret she inclined her head in grave agreement. I had wanted some reassurance. I stared across at the opposite wall which was decorated with a hanging of old Italian stamped leather, the design painted in once-brilliant tones on yellow lacquer.

"How do you know I am being followed?"

"Giorgio reported to me. He is very reliable."

"Who is Giorgio and how does he know?"

She shrugged apologetically. "It was an idea that Vernon Andrews had—just to have a man in your vicinity."

"To make sure I was not playing a double game myself?"

"Oh, I shouldn't think so. But it is routine to countercheck —certainly with Vernon. Normally of course Giorgio would have reported direct to him."

I thought this over. It would be particularly natural for a man like Andrews to have his doubts about a half-German.

"It can't be the ordinary police," I said. "It might be the O.V.R.A. What do you instruct me to do?"

She shrugged. "I can't instruct you; I can only warn you. But naturally you should carry on."

"If I have been followed it's likely to have implicated Andrews already. And you—I walked as far as the Quay with you."

"Giorgio says you have only been followed since this morning—since you went out this morning."

Silence fell. In a sense we were both leaderless, groping. The shock, the first shock, was moving out of me but leaving behind an utter certainty of failure, of the ruin of all our rash and sanguine plans. I looked at her. She was staring down at her sandals, face hidden. She should have been a temporary distraction from imminence of disaster. In a sense she was. But perhaps there was not enough of the sanguine Englishman in me to struggle with the older, more realistic Austrian.

"How did you come to be connected with this work?"

"Well . . ."

"But no doubt that is the wrong question to put in this service."

She smiled. "I'm an Australian; Andrews told you that, didn't he? I came over in July, thirty-seven, to see my father's grave; he was killed in the last war. That fall I met Paul Howard in Paris. He was in a bank there. We got married. After a while things didn't go so well between us, and when he was transferred to Italy, I stayed on in Paris. I was in Paris when war was declared."

She lit another cigarette from the butt of the old. Mine was only half through.

"I thought first of going back home to Sydney; three brothers run my father's farm; but then I heard two of them had joined the R.A.A.F., so I thought I'd stay on in Europe to see if I could help in some way—a hospital maybe, or driving an ambulance. Then someone learned that Paul was living in Venice and it was suggested that I should join him and help in another way."

"Does he know what you are doing and approve of it?"

"Oh yes. Oh, yes. He's quite a nice guy. Even though we don't hit it off much as husband and wife."

"So he does not care what risks you run?"

"It's my own life. But I wouldn't say the risks are all that great. My American citizenship is some protection, and really I only do small things. And sometimes I carry messages to and from Milan."

That hint of drawl in her voice. She called it 'Stralia, and J'ly, and Parus. And speaking of Monday and other days of the week, the accent was equal on both syllables instead of on the first.

She was highly strung and she smoked too much.

How old—twenty-five?—Australian women were very self-reliant. Did her husband know of her affair with Vernon Andrews? Clearly he didn't care anyway. Why should I?

So this feeling was something else. Something very irrelevant to a man in my position, a spy spied upon, liable at any time to be arrested and shot.

She said: "Sorry, I've not offered you a drink." It was as if some perception in her had become aware of what I was thinking. Certainly nothing was said, nothing scarcely looked, but somehow she knew, and I knew she knew.

"Strega, or cognac? Or we have a little Scotch."

"Cognac. Thank you. Does your husband know I was coming?"

"He's out. He spends two or three evenings a week at the Casino."

"Perhaps I should leave before he comes home."

"Not unless you want to."

"I don't want to."

"Then I'll fix you a drink."

While she was doing it I began to examine the sculptured head of a woman with face upturned, on the bookcase beside me. This was modern, directly molded in terra cotta, slightly stained.

"And you, Dr. Mencken. Why did you volunteer for this work?"

"I did not. The initiative came from the government. I'm not an adventurous man."

"Your father was an anti-Nazi?"

"Well, he died in a concentration camp."

"I'm sorry."

I touched the top of the molded head. The face seemed to have the strained youthfulness of a death mask.

"He was one of the old Liberals, you understand. His ideas belonged to the nineteenth century, when almost everyone accepted the proposition that humanity was perfectible and was in the process of perfecting itself. To him the dignity and importance of the individual were all. How could he help but be anti-Nazi, though in the mildest, most gentle way? They arrested him the day Hitler entered Vienna. He spent two months in a camp near Linz. They notified us he had died of appendicitis. A friend told me the truth. I wish he had not. They had nothing actually against me, and with the help of the Quakers we were permitted to leave, my mother, my sister and myself. When we reached England my mother's brother helped us. I got work in a university and things went well until I was interned in May. That is all."

She came away from the scarlet curtains, which had been a good background for her, handed me a glass with a half smile. "Drink this."

I did so, half in a draft. I needed it.

"They shouldn't have asked you to do a job like this," she said.

"Why not?"

"Well, you've been through it all once."

"No doubt it is all the more reason why I should be able to do this work."

She frowned at her glass. "What I mean is, once you've been under an oppression, it needs much more resolution to come back, knowing what it's like."

"I see my pretense of courage has not deceived you."

"It isn't a *pretense* of courage."

I shrugged. "Perhaps to be a success as a spy one *must* have something of the continental outlook. It may be harder to come back, one may be less brave because of it; but half one's value is in having it. That's why Andrews, no doubt, is such a success." I had brought his name in deliberately.

"He's Welsh," she said. "It seems strange, though I suppose it's really not so strange, that you look more English than he does."

This remark gratified me very much—not so much because I mind which race I resemble but because she had said it.

Just being with her kept the fear and the encroaching danger a finger's breadth away.

It did not even seem to matter that she was having this affair with Andrews. That was unreal. What was real was the temporary oasis of our being together now.

She had been to Vienna but not before the German occupation. I told her about the murder of Dollfuss, the betrayal of Schuschnigg, the suicide of Fey. Time passed so quickly that it was almost eleven when a footstep outside brought me to my feet.

"It's all right," she said. "I reckon it's only Paul."

A tall balding man of about thirty-five came in. He had prominent eyes and a quiet manner.

"Infernal luck tonight—" then he saw me. "Sorry. Am I intruding?"

Jane Howard said: "This is Signor Catania. My husband."

"Glad to know you," he said briefly. "What's the time, Jane? My watch stopped and—"

"Signor Catania," said his wife, "is one of us."

"Oh," said Mr. Howard, and offered a large bony rather damp hand. "That's different. The *zanzares* were troubling me on the steamboat, Jane. Have you that lotion stuff? What part of the world do you come from, *signore*? One drawback to this place—"

"Near London." Everyone else was being frank.

He looked at me with new interest. "London, England?"

"Yes."

"By the Lord God, that's a change anyway. How did you get here? No, don't tell me, I'm not supposed to know anything. Citizen of a neutral country, so they say. Tell me one thing, how are they taking the bombing over there?"

"Very well."

"Not cowering in terror the way some of these papers say? Some of your boys were over here last month. Missed the

Arsenal by a hundred yards. That's the way of bombing: it's like roulette: you stake on fourteen and thirteen comes up. There was a girl there tonight couldn't go wrong. Sheer luck, no system in it. Do you ever play roulette?"

"Never seriously, I'm afraid."

"No game is ever worth playing if you don't play it seriously. That's the trouble with you British. You didn't take Hitler seriously till it was nearly too late. Still . . . you've got guts and the English Channel. I've laid two to one that you win in the end."

"It will be a pleasure not to disappoint you," I said.

"And three to one that America's in the war by next June. Have you found the lotion, Jane? Remember, you had it last."

"It's in the bathroom," she said, and fetched it, together with a fur cape. "I'll walk back part way with you," she said to me.

I half began to protest, but my own wishes were too definite to put much weight into it.

"I need the walk," she said to Howard. "I'll not be long."

"O.K. I'm going to bed." The last I saw of him he was standing before a mirror dabbing with some lotion at the back of his neck.

We left as I had come, but instead of taking a gondola walked along a three-foot-wide path to join an alley which led into a long narrow street. Light from the shrouded moon was sufficient to show the way. There seemed not to be a soul about. With the growing of the moon the risk of bombing increased.

We did not speak. There was something between us, grown between us and still growing. Yet we both knew perfectly well that there was no foreseeable future in it. As I have said, there is a pessimistic streak in me that I remember in my own grandfather. It is probably a Viennese characteris-

tic—along with the tinsel joy of the Strauss waltz there is
always the fatalistic beat of a death-wish—and I knew from
what she had said tonight that my mission was almost certainly doomed to failure. If I reached the conference at all I
was likely to be pounced on immediately afterward. This
awareness, this sense of futility, must surely have been common to us both; but like a sudden tropical heat it warmed the
seed of our attraction and forced it into rapid growth. The
condemned man may have no place in his attention for sexual
attraction, but the part-condemned man can; I know, for it
happened to me.

"I have lost my way," I said, and meant it symbolically as
well as in fact.

"We're making for the Accademia Bridge. I'll come that far.
I love walking in Venice at night."

"I love walking in Venice at any time."

"But at night it's different. Then it's back in its great days.
The busiest port in the world. The center of culture. Full of
merchant princes and beautiful women. Glittering lights and
golden palaces and lantern-lit gondolas."

"All the beautiful women have not gone."

She said: "Isn't it the first time ever that the people of
Venice have been at war with the British?"

"I am not sure even now that they are in their hearts. A
Venetian always seems to be a Venetian first and an Italian
afterward."

"Like a Viennese in Austria?" she suggested mischievously.

"Possibly so."

"It's such a queer war. It's not really a war of nations at all,
is it?"

"You think not?"

"Paul says not. He says it's a war of religion—and of
creeds."

73

"In this disbelieving age? . . . He is probably right. But I wonder whether religion will survive it."

"You're not a religious man, Robert?"

"I? . . . I don't know. My father was. I am not in that way."

We had reached the open space before the art gallery and the old black wooden bridge of the Accademia. I realized more than ever that once she had turned back, nothing remained for me but the dark.

"Vernon will be home tomorrow forenoon," she said. "If he wants to send you a message . . . the telephone is dangerous. Go to Giorgio . . . We call him that because he looks after the San Giorgio dei Greci Church and pesters everyone to let him show them round. Go there tomorrow at six, and if we have a message for you we'll leave it with him."

"Very well," I said.

We had walked halfway across the bridge. Here on a night of peace all the brightness of the Grand Canal would show, glittering like a golden snake. Tonight there was nothing. The moon, more than half hidden, cast a gray shimmering smear over the canal like a reflection on an unpolished shield. Here and there subdued lights winked in the hotels. A great canopy of cloud lay over the city like a circus tent. It was very still, very quiet, no footsteps, no wind, no echoing voices.

"That's all then . . . Robert. Good luck."

We stood there a minute or so in the warm dark. I put my hands on her shoulders.

"You have been a lot of help."

"Help? I wish I could help more practically."

"You can."

Back against the parapet of the bridge. Lips. Jasmine. Smooth cheek. Lips curiously fresh, unspoiled, as if never touched before—by Vernon Andrews, by Paul Howard, by anyone but Robert Mencken, the fool. Body against mine,

74

very slight, boneless, full of promise. Lips. She moved her face away to breathe but I followed it. Face pale in moon, unformed, female, beautiful, full of promise.

I put my head on her shoulders, nose against her neck, breathing deeply.

"Jane."

"Take care," she said. "This is a romantic city."

"I do not feel romantic."

"No," she said after a minute. "Neither do I."

"When can we meet again?"

"I don't know. How can we plan?"

Someone was coming across the bridge. It was a policeman. I held her close. He came slowly, his feet heavy, pacing, taking his time. As he neared us, one of the larger vaporettos slid under the bridge: the pulsing of its engines, the sound of murmured voices on it, drowned his footsteps. When it had gone there were no footsteps. I lifted my head an inch and saw him leaning over the opposite parapet watching the boat draw in toward the Maria del Giglio stop. After a minute he straightened up and went on his way.

"It's not wise to linger here," she said.

"You must go back?"

"I must go back. We can't afford to take risks."

I wondered which risks she meant: they were so varied and so many. "How can we meet?" I said.

"I might be in Milan; I sometimes carry messages. But we can't plan."

"No," I said, my face against hers. "We can't plan."

I do not recall much of the solitary walk home except, near the hotel, reluctant to come under surveillance again, I stopped at a wine shop and sat down in the smoky warmth next to a gondolier with gold earrings who wanted to tell me some story of a quarrel he had just had.

Since a month, my world had been inchoate—scientist-pacifist-turned-spy made no reliable sense; but now while in the process of moving with the inevitability of Greek tragedy toward imprisonment and death, I was initiating, if it were at all possible, an affair with the mistress of the chief British agent in the area. This made nonsense by any standard: it would have been calculated idiocy for a practised roué; how much more so for a man of retiring habits with academic but little other experience.

I was a fool, of course, masterfully overtaken by a mouth and eyes and a lovely skin and a scent of jasmine. She had been right to warn me of the dangers of romantic self-deception. There was also the danger that a love affair, even of the most innocent kind, would confuse judgment and undermine my courage.

"Mind you," said the gondolier, "at the outset I addressed him politely. 'Luigi,' I said, 'Luigi Martelli, you must know that I have stood in this place these ten months past, and my father before me. Fair is fair, and I must ask you to move.' He refused, *signore*, and in the heat of the argument that followed he called me the son of a bitch."

Now I was tired and without hope. Suddenly I could perceive how pathetic the delusion was, how body and mind, threatened in their integrity, clung to a sudden notion of romantic love as a support and an escape. So long as she was with me the fantasy was just conceivable. As soon as she was gone the very frame collapsed. I knew the truth and already had no reserves to face it.

"The tale is not finished yet, *signore*," said the gondolier, clutching my arm as I got up. "As yet there is no ending. After this pig, this Martelli, had climbed out of the canal, he saw fit to report me to the police—"

But I had bowed to him and left. I wished I had had the recklessness to get drunk; but nothing must blur the faculties now; I did not know what might await me round the corner at my hotel.

The old pale city was quiet in the moon-gray night, and water lapped against its ancient stone. Two cats quarreled on a nearby wall.

My thoughts were like cats: they moved in the darkness, sometimes predatory, sometimes sexual, sometimes sleek, more often fearful, always on guard. "As yet there is no ending," the gondolier had said. There never could be in this life. My father had once said: "There is no safety but death."

He had found it, and—perhaps as a true Christian should— at the hands of his enemies.

CHAPTER 8

The Church of San Giorgio dei Greci is on a canal running in from the lagoon just beyond the Bridge of Sighs. It has a leaning tower which looks as if it is going to pitch into the canal, and early the following evening I entered its cool dark interior with the air of yet another tourist doing the rounds.

The weather was still poor; only once since I arrived had I seen the lagoon its usual paint blue; and at lunch I had heard a man say there had been snow in Como.

I had been in the church barely two minutes when a small man attached himself and, finding me not too hostile, immediately took on the duties of official guide. He was a poor little specimen, with polypus and no front teeth, so that his Italian, which had a strong accent anyhow, was difficult to understand.

He explained to me that this was a Greek Orthodox church, and he took me round to see the golden crosses and the glittering ikons and the handsome doors of the inner altar.

There were one or two other people in the church praying and genuflecting, and just as a bearded priest in his black robes and high black hat came from behind the hidden altar I felt a small roll of paper pressed into my hand. I had not made myself known in any way, but had gone into the church just when the clocks were striking six, and no doubt Giorgio had been furnished with an accurate description.

We went all round the church, and he seemed in no hurry to finish his description, but at length I was able to tip him and get away. Outside I sat in a café and bought a newspaper and read about the latest Italian naval successes, and behind the pages read the note. *"Calleto Veneto, No. 3. Major Berczik. Tomorrow morning at 7. You will not be followed. Go out tonight. A long walk after 10 p.m. Destroy this."*

I rubbed the piece of paper into a ball no bigger than a pea and thought of tossing it into the convenient canal, but changed my mind. Though no one could salve it, someone might see it go. Better burned.

I stayed there a time reading the paper through, then got up and strolled quietly back toward the Hotel San Moisé. In one of the narrow streets leading to St. Mark's Square there was the usual press of people entering and leaving the piazza, and while I squeezed among them a man turned sharply to avoid someone and bumped into me.

"Vi domando perdone," he said, and raised his hat and passed on; a big man in a check suit. He spoke Italian with an accent I could not place; provoking because I prided myself. Swiss? Dutch? Perhaps even an Italian from the border regions of the Dolomites.

So they wanted me to walk. Over dinner I planned it. Venice is the only city in the world where one may go anywhere equally well by land or by water. I decided to retrace last night's route, crossing the Grand Canal by way of the Ponte dell' Accademia, and then make a great circle of the city, recrossing by the station bridge and eventually approaching St. Mark's Square from the east again.

I remembered the note should be destroyed, and after dinner went up to my room. It was only then that I found my right overcoat pocket to be entirely empty.

There had been two or three boat tickets in it, a stub of pencil, a half slab of chocolate, a restaurant bill. When I came out of the Church of San Giorgio I had put Dwight's note there. It was fortunate that later in the café, I had transferred it to an inner waistcoat pocket, where it now was.

I took it out and set a match to the corner and watched it turn black and crumble away.

Next morning the sun was streaming in on my face. From now to the end, I felt, whatever the end might be, there would be no more time for hesitation and doubt. No time for morbid fears inbred by ancestors who saw the future of the human race too clearly. Action now, not pessimism. This morning I officially became Captain Bonini's secretary. At twelve-thirty I left for Milan. At seven . . .

At five minutes to seven I was walking down the Calleta Veneto. The bad weather had gone at last and it was a perfect, sparkling morning, fresh and yet warm, the streets just drying from the night's rain. A barge was coming down the canal laden to the gunwale with vegetables and grapes. A boy was baling rainwater from his father's gondola and singing.

At five minutes after seven I was in the presence of both Dwight and Andrews. It was a more luxurious room than that in which I had twice met them before. The entrance was shabby in the extreme, like a slum, with a tattered iron-bound door and gaping dustbins on either side; but you went along a shabby passage and then came into a room looking the other way, with dignified hand-carved furniture and rich Oriental carpets.

"A good deal, old man," Dwight said, patting my shoulder with false bonhomie, "a good deal has happened since we met last week. Thought it only right to keep you up to date with the list of runners."

"Mrs. Howard told me I was being followed," I said grimly, "but I presume she told you too. So I did what you instructed and came straight here. In fact it was fortunate that that note did not fall into the wrong hands."

"How was that, old man?" Dwight's ice-blue uncommunicative eyes; his brown leathery skin tight drawn across the narrow cheek bones; the morning light was not kind to him.

"That was well done," said Andrews, from the window, when I had told them. "But in future destroy at once. Never let the risk arise."

We had hardly spoken; I thought it was as if he was somehow aware I had been poaching on his preserves.

"I don't know," I said, "how you could be certain that I was not followed here. This man who picked my pocket could have been waiting outside the hotel to see me leave."

"Well, no, he couldn't, old man," Dwight said. "That at least is fairly clear."

Andrews licked his thick lips. "We're *not* certain, Mencken, that you weren't *followed*. We can't be *certain*. But we have reason to believe that you weren't. That man, for instance, that man who bumped into you has met with an accident. Too bad. A poor type. He drank too much sour Italian wine and fell in a canal. It's easy to do in Venice. The police found his body an hour ago."

"How do you . . . Oh," I said.

There was silence. In it a fly buzzed on a window pane.

"He was not a type I admire," Andrews said.

I got up. "I see." I felt sick, lost, out of touch.

Dwight seemed to be trying to read my expression, as if he really cared what I felt. "This is war, you know. Two can play. It's a question of being a jump ahead of the other feller. National Hunt rules."

"There are no rules," Andrews said. "He fell in a canal. Can we help that?" He offered me his cigar case.

Harshly I said, no thanks. "I don't see this that you've done—or arranged to be done—I don't see how it will help for more than a few hours. If the man who is shadowing me is found to be dead, won't the police arrest me at once? Or, if that is forbidden, they will just attach another detective. We can't go on—"

"Withdrawing them from circulation," said Andrews, "that is the fashionable phrase in this country."

"You can't go on disposing of people who are put on the case. If the Italian police know all about me, there's no cure. We have simply shown our hand . . ."

Major Dwight began to cough. He coughed until the veins stood out on his neck and forehead like pipe lines. "So far the Italian police—old man—know nothing—whatever about you."

"Then who does?"

Andrews sat down opposite me. One of his fly buttons was undone and he fastened it. "Certain effects were found on the dead man. They indicate that he was not an Italian at all."

"No, probably Swiss. His accent gave him away."

". . . We won't argue. Ever heard of an address, 26, Salier Ring, Cologne?"

I shook my head.

"Or of a certain Herr Wolfram Hacker?"

"No. Was that his name?"

"No. That was the name of the man who countersigned his secret identity warrant."

"Who was he? I don't follow you."

"See, look for yourself." Andrews took from his pocket a folded sheet of stiff and rather soiled paper.

My eyes fled over the wording to the signature at the bottom. Beside the signature was the print of a rubber stamp, like a circular postmark. Inside the perimeter of the stamp were the words: *Geheime Staatspolizei*.

I cannot begin to describe the effect those words had on me. A man finding himself in an enclosed space with a deadly snake. A man suddenly told he has an incurable disease. A man without hope . . .

I went to the window in search of air.

Dwight said: "Don't take it like that, old man."

In the canal below, the boy was still baling out the gondola. The dome of a church glistened like gold in the sun.

"Of course," Dwight said, "precautions were taken to see that the Italian police found nothing on the body. Unless we're unlucky his identity won't be established for some days. We think he was a lone wolf and nobody will own him."

Blue smoke drifting across the window panes told me that Andrews had come up silently beside me.

"Chances are," Dwight said, "chances are very much that you'll have a week free of surveillance, and that'll be more than enough."

"What . . ." I stopped and began again. "What have the Gestapo to do with me?"

"We don't know, but we suspect."

"You suspect someone?"

"Bonini."

"Why?"

"For nearly a month now Bonini has been in correspondence with someone in Deutz, which is a suburb of Cologne. We think now the letters will have passed to 26, Salier Ring, which is the headquarters of the Gestapo for that division. We have never been able to get any idea of the contents."

"You mean he's betrayed us?"

"We think he's betrayed you."

"But why to Germany, when the Italian police are on his doorstep?"

Dwight came to the window, coughed into his handkerchief. "Bonini has a German wife. We thought they were completely estranged, but maybe when he was worried over this he went to her. This is a way out of his fix, d'you see. If he laid information with the Gestapo they'd solve things in their own way without anyone else knowing of his previous little betrayals. Whereas if he went to *Organizzazione Vigilanza* he'd be the first to suffer—as we've always calculated."

Solve things their own way. How often the German secret police had been given orders like that. And how often they had done so.

"If Bonini has betrayed me," I said, "he is like to have betrayed you and Andrews and Mrs. Howard. There would be no point in him taking half measures."

"Set your mind at rest about all that, old man. That's if you're really worried about us. Bonini has never even heard of me or Andrews and he knows nothing of Jane Howard's connection with you. The one most likely to suffer is our go-between, the head of the credit house. We have already warned him. But this is why they have made no hostile move against you. They wanted to catch bigger fish. A single agent wasn't enough. They hoped with a little patience they'd be able to uncover your connections. They may even vaingloriously have thought of doing it and then presenting the case to the O.V.R.A. neatly sewn up, showing their own great superiority. That's only a guess, but it's the sort of thing that's happened before."

"Otherwise," said Andrews, "it would have been your body the street sweeper found floating in the Rio Palazzo, not his."

Dwight laughed apologetically. "Well, we mustn't look on

the black side, must we. Things have not worked out too badly so far. But we did consider it only fair to you to give you the latest odds. Bonini will still be unable to refuse to take you to Milan as his secretary. He'll reason that a Gestapo man is watching you and will take comfort in that. He'll play his part knowing—or thinking he knows—that you'll be picked off his back at the right moment."

"I would think my chances of going through with this successfully are very small indeed now."

Andrews put his fat hand on my arm. "Small chances sometimes lead to great successes, Doctor. It is how one takes them. Now . . . we've made two changes of plan to try to help you. We shall *both* be in Milan at the time of the conference to try to see you through to the straight safely, as Dwight would say. We shall go up to Milan on an early train tomorrow. There shouldn't be any danger in your being unprotected tonight. That's the first change. The second is that, once the conference is over you will no longer return to Venice with Bonini for the sake of appearances but will leave Italy at the earliest possible moment and by a new route. Dwight will see to all that. You remember the address we gave you where you would go if things went wrong?"

"Yes."

"What is it?"

"Manuel Lorenza. Lorenzo e Societa, Via Monte Rosa, 11, off Corso Vittorio Emmanuele."

"Good. Well, go there in any case now—as soon as the conference is over."

"What of Bonini?"

"That," said Andrews, "we will leave until you are safely gone." He looked down at his fingers and whistled a bar or two of *Giovinezza*. "Youth, youth, thou lovely thing, time of Springtime's blossoming. Fascismo brings the promise of Freedom for the people."

"There's no place for revenge in this business," Dwight said impatiently. "Bonini we shall use or discard as suits us best. By the way, old man, there is one other thing . . ."

"Yes?"

"Did they give you anything in London before you left, to take if you were captured and things got too bad?"

"No."

"I'm surprised. Well look; this pencil; take this. The bit of indiarubber at the end; it's not indiarubber. If they take it off you, they'll always give it back to you if you say there's a message wound round the lead. Just bite it. That's all."

"Thank you," I said grimly.

"Don't worry, old man. We don't *expect* anything of the sort. But it's a precaution. If we were all caught it would hobble British activity in this area for some time."

"It's fortunate," I said, "that the Gestapo did not kidnap me right off and try to persuade me to tell them what I already know."

Dwight shook his head. "They're not playing on their own ground. And besides—as an agent, I know—it's far better to make a big haul at the first grab. Let it be known, even for an hour or so, that one fish is caught, and the others fairly *melt* into the background. *Fast.* It's surprising how fast one can move when one's life is at stake."

Shortly after this I left. My knees still felt as if all the bones had melted. I did not walk home as I would have done normally but took a gondola. I felt as short of breath as if I had been climbing a cathedral tower.

The knowledge that one is receiving the attentions of the *Geheime Staatspolizei* (foreign branch) has been known to have that effect on many other people. But not a lot of them have lived long enough to record it.

CHAPTER 9

I caught the 12:30 train to Milan.

I had had a short interview with Captain Bonini, who looked as handsome and as hostile as ever; but little came from it except curt instructions as to my duties in Milan and how I must prepare for his arrival tomorrow.

On the train all sorts of questions that I had not put to Andrews and Dwight crowded into my head. If the Gestapo lost a man, were they not likely to break their undertaking with Bonini and inform O.V.R.A. about me at once? If Bonini had been in touch direct with Gestapo headquarters, was it not also likely that he was in touch with the man they had sent to tail me? Then he would know of his disappearance almost immediately. Even worse, did *any* organization, certainly any of the known abilities of the Gestapo, send down *one* man to keep track of a suspect? Were there not almost certain to be two? How otherwise could a permanent watch be kept?

I could picture Dwight and Andrews, before I came this morning, discussing the risks and how best I could be bolstered into going on with the suicidal mission. "Well, Andrews," Dwight would say, "he was a hundred-to-one runner anyhow. Probabilities are, he'll fall now at the very first fence. Why not scratch him, get him out of the country while there's still a few hours to spare?" "No," Andrews would say, "we've got to push him through on the off chance, there's no one else to take his place, and anyway's he's expendable. He's half Kraut."

It was noticeable today that Dwight had done almost all the talking. At first I had thought that Andrews with some Celtic sixth sense had perceived my sudden interest in Jane. Now I thought otherwise: it was simply that he had made the decision to go ahead and virtually send me to my death, so he had delegated the task of persuading me to Major Dwight.

The train was very crowded, even for Italy, and I had already closely studied everyone in the compartment, wondering if any of them received their instructions from Cologne.

I also had time to wonder what my father would have said if he could see me now. He had believed that all killing was morally wrong and that the worst crime to be committed under any circumstances was the taking of life. I had imbibed these ideas early, yet had never completely accepted them. As a scientist I had found the logic of them faulty. Yet deep down some part of them still stuck, and it was a curiously uncomfortable feeling that the big German in the check suit with the turned-down velour hat had been done to death on my behalf. I had been specially asked to take a long walk in order to lure him into a dark byway of the city. This was somehow more personal than fifty people killed in an air raid. I felt I had had a hand in it, as if I had helped to strike the blow. That he would have done the same to me without the slightest compunction still did not absolve me from responsibility.

Perhaps it was only time before these sentimental elements were finally purged away. Logically, why should one not feel exultation at this turning of the tables, at this deliberate destruction of a man who represented a body responsible for the greatest number of murders in civilized history? Every other terrorism that had existed was milk and water to this. Compared to it, the Spanish Inquisition had been as lethal as little children playing shop. It was a change at least to be in the company of someone who played the same game. In Austria there had *never* been any appeal against the Gestapo, *never* any court of redress, never any real danger to *them*. I should be *glad* for what had happened, even if the mental acceptance of it was a step toward de-civilization. The world had long since outstripped me on this path.

The Hotel Colleoni in Milan is in the Viale Vittorio Veneto overlooking the public gardens. As my taxi drew up at the door a squadron of three-engined Caproni aircraft roared low overhead. The taxi driver looked up querulously and said: "Will they never leave us in peace and quiet?"

Later I learned that British bombers had been over last night; but the driver's complaint seemed directed against war and airplanes in general.

The reserved rooms were on the first floor with balconies looking out on the gardens. The other room would be occupied by Captain Bonini tomorrow.

By the time I had settled in it was dark, but I caught a tram as far as the Scala Theatre and walked round the center of the town and dined at Biffis. I had already located Lorenzo and Co. in the Via Monte Rosa, a good class dress shop with a department for men; and it was some comfort to know exactly where my bolt-hole was.

I did not go into the main restaurant but ate the meal at one of the tables in the arcade. I had come to this place for the sake of being with company, but while drinking a liqueur afterward I saw Forni, the manager of the Hôtel du Sud, where I had been accustomed to stay, pass near the table. I rose quickly and paid the bill and left, suddenly anxious to change the half dark of the arcade for the blackout of the streets.

But even the streets were not dark. A full moon was rising mistily after a perfect day. It made a pale corona of light silhouetting the hundred and thirty spires of the great marble and granite cathedral. Considering it was not late there were few people about.

I decided to walk back to the hotel.

It was no distance, a kilometer or so, and would have been a pleasant walk if only, halfway, I had not become certain I was being followed.

Nerves, of course. Nerves can do so much. It is like trying to convince oneself that the half-felt pain is not there at all. Footsteps on the shadowy half-lit pavements. Why not? Other people lived here. This was not a town of the dead.

Are there some footsteps connected with me and some footsteps unconnected? (After all it is simply that the pain has been in that place before, even though that was before the operation.)

The single-decker trams clanged past, and once I almost climbed aboard at a stop. But I was playing a game in which one could not afford to be stampeded. It was now a matter of pride. One can be stiff-necked, whether Austrian or English. Plod on. Keep your nerve.

I thought how beautiful Venice would look in the growing moonlight, and wondered about Jane Howard. Already I had thought so much of our meeting and of our last parting that there did not seem to be any true emotion left; every bit had been squeezed dry. I needed to see her again to renew even my memory.

I came to a stop and bent over a shoelace. Somewhere behind me footsteps stopped also.

So it was true, the worst had happened. The dead man had not been alone in Venice. When his compatriot did not turn up the second man would have reported him as missing to some secret *Polizeihauptwachtmeister* higher up, who would telephone instructions that I should be picked up in Milan as I left the train. What more simple?

My throat was thick and dry as I straightened up, glanced casually behind, walked on. At the last corner a group of three men were talking. They had not been there when I passed.

I lengthened my stride. A hundred meters to the first of the blocks of modern flats at the corner of the square from which opened the Viale Vittorio Veneto. Five minutes to the hotel. If they were so disposed they could pick me up in that time, or, if they felt like it, with a rifle pick me off. My back already felt the sharp pain.

Across the square. If they were going to move it would have to be now. Another tram. In the moonlit sky three searchlights came secretly into existence, moved backward and forward among the faint stars. The great moon showed suddenly like an eye between the blocks of flats. Women were chattering here. Almost safety.

As I reached the hotel the three searchlights winked one by one and disappeared.

I entered and went straight upstairs. My bedroom was undisturbed.

Before getting into bed I slid the bolt across the door,

switched off the light, parted the curtains to look out. There was the square-built figure of a man standing near the entrance to the hotel waiting for a tram. But I saw three trams draw up and he did not board them.

CHAPTER 10

I woke with the rumble of the trams still in my ears. It was pitch dark in the room because the blackout was drawn, and the thick curtains made the room heavy with warmth. Having gone to sleep uneasily I was immediately and sharply awake wondering if the sound was inside the room. But all was quiet now.

Not a tram: too heavy for that. Thunder, probably; one of those sharp electric storms that brew over Milan. There was a flicker of light through the curtain and I got up to make sure. Halfway to the window I heard the drone of an airplane.

I stepped out on to the balcony.

The sky was alive with searchlights, moving, probing, flicking here and there. In the distance was the great orange glow of a fire. It was the flashes of the antiaircraft guns I had seen, and perhaps it was this noise that had wakened me. Over all the moon, now fully risen, and shrunk in size, flooded the earth with its cold light. The man who had been waiting for the tram was no longer there. It was two o'clock.

Somewhere overhead, presumably, were men who spoke my mother's tongue, who had flown seven hundred miles to make this attack and, if fortunate, would fly the same distance back again.

The focus of the raid appeared to be on the outskirts of the city. The night was mild and I got my dressing gown to watch. Some other people were doing the same, but presently the ack-ack fire grew more intense and a big gun opened up in the gardens opposite. People melted away rapidly as pieces of shrapnel began to fall.

In the corridor voices were raised. A man shouted, urging the others to "take shelter in the trenches!" Another was shouting something quite different, and an argument and hysterical voices grew up. Then close above us came the fierce drone of an airplane swooping low and climbing away again. When it had gone the voices had stopped. I looked out and saw a magnesium flare burning whitely on the tram lines.

In the corridor a woman screamed: *"Per vergogna! Non lo posso tollerare di piu!"*

After a few minutes things died down. The searchlights were still sweeping the sky and the fire still burning but the guns had stopped. Their first salvoes must have wakened me. Since I had slept through any air-raid warning there might have been, I waited to see if there was an all clear. But in half an hour the distant drone of planes could be heard again. During this second attack I sat on the bed and smoked a cigarette. Although this brief raid was nearer, I felt no fear. I expected, perhaps, that the bombs would be able to discriminate on whom they fell . . .

I tried to guess the number of planes from the sound. I should have estimated about six or seven in each flight. I decided to get dressed, for pajamas are not the best sort of shelter suit. Then I smoked another cigarette.

The gunfire ceased, this time it seemed for good. I waited twenty minutes, then began to untie my tie. As I did so the telephone on the table rang. I took off the receiver thinking it likely to be some inquiry or reassurance from the management.

"I wish to speak to Captain Bonini," said a voice.

I hesitated. "Captain Bonini is not here."

"Who is that?"

"Captain Bonini's private secretary."

"Where can I get in touch with him?"

"He is in Venice. Who is that, please?"

"Professor Brayda's secretary. I understood Captain Bonini was in Milan."

Professor Brayda. The man whose work I was to have the privilege of . . . "He is traveling up by the early train in the morning. Can I give him a message for you?"

There was a pause on the wire and it seemed to go dead.

"What is wrong?" I insisted. "I am completely in Captain Bonini's confidence."

This time I could hear whispered voices at the other end.

"Hullo."

"Hullo."

"This is Professor Brayda's secretary. Why is Captain Bonini not in Milan?"

"He had business which kept him in Venice. He is coming by the morning train. What is your message?"

"It is not a message. Professor Brayda's house and laboratory have been destroyed by a bomb. We are anxious to get in touch with those who were to have attended the conference."

Who *were* to have attended? "That is tragedy!" I said. "Is Professor Brayda safe?"

"No. Seriously injured. Good-by."

"One moment!" I said sharply.

"Well?"

"I shall be glad to come myself. Perhaps I can be of use."

"You can be of no use. Professor Brayda wishes only to get in touch with the principals. Thank you."

"I was to have attended the conference," I shouted, "I am fully empowered in every way . . . Hullo!"

The line was dead.

In the distance airplanes were droning again.

I groped a way downstairs into the wide vestibule of the hall. The light of the moon falling through the big glass porch showed the hall gray-white and deserted. The guns were firing again but raggedly as if more from routine than from conviction.

A figure moved suddenly in the shadows behind the counter, and I saw it was the porter, a lithe dark elderly man with graying sidewhiskers and sleek greasy hair.

"*Madonna!*" he exclaimed. "I thought everyone was sheltering in the basement, *signore*."

I wondered what his business was behind the reception desk.

"Are the trams still running?"

"Trams, *signore*? No, no."

"Would there be a taxi to be found?"

He made a face. "Most unlikely. Why should anyone wish to go out in this? You should go into the basement like the rest."

"I have just heard that a great friend of mine has been seriously injured. I must go to him at once."

He clicked his tongue several times. "I feel as you feel, *signore*. But why become a casualty yourself?"

"The air raid is over. Is there a hotel car I could hire?"

"There is the hotel bus. But I have no authority to loan you that. If you were to ask the proprietor—"

"There is no time. This is most urgent. Have you the authority to drive me?"

The whites of his eyes showed. "If I had the authority I should not have the inclination. Thank you."

"There would be a hundred lire for yourself."

He turned his head and listened. "Perhaps the air raid *is* over. I will go and see."

I waited. He came back. "I will pick you up at the front door in three minutes."

Another wait in the warm gray hall. There was no one else at all about. The faint purr of an engine among the other noises took me down the steps. An old Fiat with a box-shaped body to convey guests to and from the station.

Searchlights were sweeping the sky, circling the face of the moon. I climbed in beside the man.

"Where to?" he asked.

"Where would they take air-raid casualties?"

"Oh . . . it would depend on the district. The Ospedale Maggiore. Or even the military hospital." He stopped and stared at me in the dark. "But, *signore*, you do not *know* where your friend is?"

"The people who telephoned rang off before I could ask."

"Do you tell me we are to go from hospital to hospital inquiring, while overhead—"

"No, we'll go to his house. That is close to the Faroni works. You know the way?"

He jumped. "Mother of God! You ask me to drive just where they are dropping the bombs? You can keep your hundred lire!"

I grabbed his arm as he moved to get out. "Two hundred for a successful drive. It is nothing. The raid is over."

"I do not know the direction by night," he said sulkily.

I smiled unpleasantly in the darkness. "All you have to do is make for the fire."

We sat together in silence. The last gun had ceased. A great silence reigned.

"Very well, if you insist. I do not know what the manager will say, risking his bus."

We drove off. The man used only sidelights and mainly stayed in third gear, with his foot hard down on the accelerator and his finger on the horn. On any straight road we went flat out. Even in the moonlight there was much that was deceptive.

We roared through deserted streets, tires screeching at corners, horn blaring our coming. We narrowly missed an ambulance and a fire engine. At least it seemed unlikely that anyone could possibly follow us. Unless, sneaking fear, the message was a decoy.

We flashed into open country, whirred between vineyards down a wide white autostrada, cleft with a sensation of impact the next mound of shadow. We were among villas again. Ahead lay the straggling bulk of the great Faroni works. On the right was the fire.

A steel-helmeted policeman barred our way. We squealed and jerked to a standstill.

"No way through. Make a detour by way of—"

"Professor Brayda's house!" I shouted. "Which way is that?"

"Professor Brayda's house has been bombed. You can't come through."

"I must see Professor Brayda at once. Is he still here?"

The policeman cocked a wary eye at the sky. "They're coming back again. What is your business?"

"Urgent message from Captain Bonini of the Naval Staff."

"Very well. Go on. Sharp right at the next turning, and then on the left twenty yards from where the road is blocked."

My chauffeur lifted an eyebrow at me as we drove on. "Is it true? About this Captain, you know—"

"Of course it's true. Careful!"

We passed a group of people and then, turning left as directed, came on imposing gates, of which one was open. My driver was inclined to stop, but I prodded him to drive on, and no one came out to interfere. The blaze was over on the right; a group of buildings was burning separate from the main factory. Ahead were more houses.

Our car came to another screeching halt. "We cannot go on. The road is thick with glass."

The drone of airplanes. I gave the man a hundred lire note and got out. "Draw in to the side and wait for me. I'll not be long. If bombing starts take shelter under the car."

He began to protest but I left him there, ran across to the houses, the glass crunching like ice underfoot. Two of the houses were not much more than heaps of rubble, a third had the roof and one wall missing.

Fireman carrying a length of hose: I caught his arm. "Professor Brayda's house?"

His face gleamed yellow in the fireglow; he nodded without speaking to the third house. I ran toward it. No one about. Now the guns were opening up afresh; it would soon be unhealthy out of doors. The last house on the left was undamaged except for broken windows. A man answered my heavy knock.

"Can you tell me where they have taken Professor Brayda?" I asked.

"He's here. What do you want?"

Luck. "I want to see him."

"Nobody can see him. He's badly injured."

"But I am here at his special request. You telephoned me."

Hesitation on the man's face. "Are you one of the scientists? We couldn't get hold of them."

"I represent Captain Bonini. I was to have attended tomorrow's conference on behalf of the Admiralty."

"Oh, well." A piece of antiaircraft shell hit the railings near us with a clang. "You'd better come in."

I followed him down a long hall to the foot of the stairs. "I will inquire," he said.

Why had they wanted so urgently to get in touch with the scientists tonight? Instead of waiting I followed the man up the stairs.

At the top he was talking with a man who had a stained bandage round his head. They both stared at me. Before they could object I again said who I was. "I was given instructions to take all responsibility for Captain Bonini, just as if he were here. When someone telephoned me—"

"I telephoned," said the wounded man.

"When you telephoned and suggested I should come—"

"I? I suggested no such thing. You—"

"But you *did*. Did you not say—"

"Oh, there is some mistake." The man turned away wearily. "Anyway, since you had the courage to come, see Professor Brayda if it pleases you. It can do him no harm."

"In here," said the man who had admitted me, opening a door.

Large bedroom, pleasantly furnished in a style fashionable before the First World War. Six people. On the edge of an easy chair a stout elderly woman sat weeping, her hair hanging in gray wisps. Sitting beside the bed was a man whose tonsure showed that when properly dressed he would have worn a cassock; his eyes, nearly closed, showed a thin slit of pale iris; he was intoning in Latin. The sound went on without a break all the time I was in the room.

"Yes, gentlemen," said a voice. "But there are graver

potentialities in this than you'd think . . . If someone can demonstrate . . . aftereffects are quite clear . . ."

It was the man on the bed who spoke, in a weak slurred voice. Handsome, about sixty, with an imperial and a short mustache. His eyes were open, but there was no comprehension in them. Professor Brayda, the man for whom I had come the length of Europe. . . .

No one paid attention to me and I approached the bed.

"Concentration of one to a million, with something like a thirty minutes exposure. You will see from this . . ."

I glanced at the weeping woman. This was the lowest common denominator of war. Weeping women all over the earth. This was the final insanity. Nationality did not count for much when it came down to individuals. We all had the same measuring stick of sorrow.

"*Quia tu es, Deus, fortitudo mea, quare me repulisti? Et quare tristis incedo dum affligit me inimicus?*"

One of the three men near the bed suddenly said to me: "What is it that you want?"

"I represent the Admiralty. Professor Brayda is . . . ?"

"Nothing at all can be done. The wall fell on him." The speaker turned again to the dying man, taking his wrist between thumb and forefinger. "I am needed urgently elsewhere," he said, relinquishing the wrist. "Signora Brayda, you understand? As there is nothing, nothing to be done here I cannot afford to stay. In other circumstances, of course . . ."

The woman nodded without speaking.

"And I must go too," said one of the other men. "Listen to that! They are bombing again. They shall pay for this! Have no fear, Signora Brayda, they shall pay for this! You shall be revenged. Their cities shall be burned to the ground!" He followed the physician to the door. "You are staying, Dr. von Riehl?"

I glanced sharply at the third man, who now nodded. "A little while longer," he said in awkward Italian. "Outside there is nothing I can do."

"Very well. I will return, Signora Brayda. God give you strength."

They went out. The German folded some sheets of paper on which he had been writing and put them in his pocket.

"*Domine, non sum dignus ut intres sub tectum meum,*" came the priest's low voice. "*Sed tantum dic verbo, et sanabitur anima mea.*"

I stared sidelong at Dr. Amadeus von Riehl, that highly-placed representative of the Third Reich, who was to have attended tomorrow. A man of middle age, tall and big boned, with a flushed color, hair so close cut as to merge into baldness, spectacles half-moon shape. In his buttonhole was an *Ehrenzeichen*, a Nazi long-service badge of honor.

The priest stopped his mutterings. "He wishes to speak."

At once Signora Brayda was beside the bed, wetting the sheet with her tears. Von Riehl was on the other side; I stood at the foot.

But Professor Brayda was now too far gone to recognize us. He was talking, but they were disconnected sentences, quite rational in themselves but out of context. Sometimes it seemed he was beginning a lecture, part of the address he would have given tomorrow. Sometimes he was instructing an assistant. Presently he was silent, and I thought he was gone. Dr. von Riehl put away his pencil.

But then Brayda began again. He was back with tomorrow's lecture. It seemed that he expected a certain amount of criticism on ethical grounds. He apologized that his conclusions were incomplete, but with Italy at war he felt it necessary and patriotic that his researches so far should be given this airing. The scientist was the uncommitted explorer; what he discovered might be truly put to the service of the state; but in its first stage it was no more and no less than the detached activity of the humanist brain directed toward no specific end-product. One worked, one found, one published or stated the findings: it was for the nation or the state then to decide if or how those findings should be used.

"Our distinguished visitor, Dr. von Riehl," said the injured man, and waited, as if expecting applause. "Representing our comrades in arms, the great German nation . . . with whom . . . shoulder to shoulder . . ."

"This is a great tragedy," I said in an undertone to the German. "How did it happen?"

He looked at me as if I were an impertinent servant. "As you would expect. Incendiaries on the laboratory fell. Professor Brayda and his chief assistant went to put them out. A high explosive bomb dropped, killing the assistant outright, and Brayda was crushed by a falling wall."

"Hush," said the priest. "He is going now."

The professor's wife leaned forward. His lips were working feebly, but not with any loving message of farewell. I caught the words: "Vesicant . . . less arsenic content . . . cannot be used . . . intended to occupy . . . impregnation . . . uncalculated aftereffects." Then he said: ". . . *et dimitte nobis debita nostra, sicut et nos dimittimus debitoribus nostris . . .*"

His lips fluttered and he gave a deep sigh and was still.

The priest crossed himself, and we all followed suit.

"*Agnus Dei, qui tollis peccata mundi . . .*"

Strange the silence that had fallen. It is the inexplicable silence of death. I turned away. There was nothing more here that concerned the war or the whims of dictators or the vagaries of patriotism.

I quietly left the room.

As I got to the head of the stairs there were voices at the bottom, and I saw Professor Brayda's secretary talking to a self-important but pleasant faced little man in—of all things—a morning suit.

"I ventured out as soon as ever the worst was over. Though even yet it is not safe, and, *Santa Maria*, to drive for six miles with bombs raining down on the roads! . . . Let me go up, I may be able to help him."

"I think it is too late," said the secretary.

"Well, where are the others? You did not tell me over the phone that Emilio Brayda was dying!"

"Three of the others are not yet in Milan and four have not come. Captain Bonini's secretary came; and Dr. von Riehl, who was staying near, was here almost at once . . ."

"The German? Where is he, then? I will meet him."

They saw me. The secretary explained who I was. "Professor Brayda is dead," I said.

Nobody spoke. The newcomer shook his head. "Oh, the loss! Oh, the loss for Italy!"

The man who had let me in was near by and said: "So far we have gained nothing out of this war. Not even Bizerta! Only bombs."

"Hush, it is not your place to criticize! The rewards of endurance will come later. I greatly regret my distinguished colleague's death. If Dr. von Riehl was present . . ."

A footstep behind me.

The secretary drew himself up. "Dr. von Riehl. Dr. Pietro of the University of Turin."

I moved a little away but not so far as to be unable to hear their conversation.

"A tragic evening, Dr. von Riehl. Much, much our worst raid so far."

"It was nothing to what we have given them. And shall give them in the future. But you have the loss of Herr Professor Brayda unfortunately suffered."

"This is a very grievous blow to science. His was an original mind, a lonely mind, seldom sharing his ideas. A practical eccentric, one might say. It was fortunate you were staying near. I was delayed; the police advised me it was not safe to leave the hotel."

"Quite so," rather contemptuously. "I understand. But to myself I do not think any good fortune for being at the scene of the bombing."

"I mean, in the matter of Professor Brayda's researches into the new gases."

"I am not following."

"Well, as I have said, his was always a lonely mind. If his chief assistant was killed and his laboratory wrecked, there might have been some risk at least of his latest ideas dying with him."

Von Riehl took off his half-moon glasses and breathed on them and polished them with a cream silk handkerchief.

"Yes, naturally. That too was in Professor Brayda's mind." To the secretary: "He spoke to me at some length."

"Yes, sir, I heard him. You have the notes, sir."

"I took notes," said von Riehl. "For it seemed necessary a dying man's every word to take down. It seems from what he said that this idea of his is of an irritant gas of some potential." He put his spectacles on again, hooking them carefully behind each ear. "So far so good. But in detail he spoke nothing I could understand. His brain, you see, was then wandering. A dying man's delirium."

"But, sir," the secretary said, "at first he seemed—completely himself. He spoke, I thought, very clearly, very deliberately, sir. I am not, of course, a scientist, but I have worked for Professor Brayda for three years, and—and . . ."

Dr. von Riehl looked over the top of his glasses at the wounded man. "You will see the notes? You would wish to see the notes I took?" He brought some sheets of paper from his pocket and thrust them at the secretary, who flushed and hesitantly accepted them and then without looking at them passed them to Dr. Pietro.

The Italian held them near the light and frowned.

"These are—I can make very little of this." He turned the first sheet over. "Now this is to do with hydroelectric power . . . and has some reference to deliveries of wolfram . . ."

Outside a hooter sounded; presumably the all-clear.

Dr. Pietro shook his head. "Incomprehensible. These might be supply problems. But even then much of it—you use a shorthand system, Dr. von Riehl?"

"No. But it was jotted down, you understand, in haste. Often his words no sense made. Like a child, delirious."

The Italian shrugged. "This is too bad. Well . . . first I must pay my sad respects to his widow. Then the laboratory. What can be salvaged—"

"Have you seen it?" the secretary asked.

"As bad as that? But surely he kept notes of his work? Full notes."

"Yes, full notes in his office, I know. But that received the direct hit."

"Anyway we shall try. Perhaps we shall be allowed a small light now. Then in the morning a thorough search. Where did he keep his personal papers?"

"In the house next door, sir. His house. But they were chiefly personal. I did not deal with his scientific findings."

Dr. von Riehl picked up his hat. "He was to me most anxious the information to impart. Unfortunate to fail."

"Unfortunate indeed," said Pietro. "I met him at a small scientific party two months ago in Turin and he gave me then the impression that his work was exciting him—even alarming him."

"Too bad. Too bad."

I did not want to leave with von Riehl so I slipped out of

the house ahead of him. I had been very lucky all through, and one did not want to try one's luck too far.

In only one thing had I been very unfortunate, and that was in not being on the scene half an hour earlier. Then I could have been sure to what extent von Riehl was lying.

I was certain he was lying for two reasons. He had taken the notes from a different pocket from that in which I had seen him put them. And although Brayda's mind may have been confused by the approach of death when I was present, he had spoken sensibly enough to give me the gist of what he had probably told Dr. Amadeus von Riehl. And there was nothing nonsensical in that.

CHAPTER 11

There were a number of simple choices I could have made at this time, and of all of them I no doubt chose the unwisest. But I had left my papers and my passport at the hotel, and it seemed to me that the only course was to go back for them and then ring Andrews, so that if he gave me different instructions I could act on them without, if need be, any later return. Of course I knew that my headlong drive to the Faroni works had almost certainly rid me of any followers, and by going back I might run into them again; but in any event I was still officially Edmondo Catania attached to Captain Bonini, and perhaps should have to continue to behave like him.

When I got back to the hotel I paid off the driver and went in. There was no one about, and my bedroom was again untouched, the bed still with the impression of my body on it. Telephone Andrews from here? That seemed unwise. Wait until morning? But Andrews and Dwight were leaving by the early train.

I stuffed papers and passport in my pocket, walked quietly out on to the balcony. Almost below, to the left of the hotel door, a square-built hatless man in a raincoat was standing.

It was now after four o'clock. Where was the nearest public telephone? The station was not very far away: a five- or six-minute walk. One could probably telephone in perfect safety from there.

But could one *walk* in perfect safety? The trams, I thought, did not start till six. The chance of a taxi was small. But if this man who followed me had wanted to, he could have killed me last night.

There was a tired dark man behind the reception desk now, but he only raised tired dark eyes as I passed. As I came out I had to turn left, away from where the man in the raincoat would still be standing. I walked off at a brisk pace in the direction of the Stazione Centrale.

There was no one at all about; Milan was making up for its disturbed night. I did not turn, though once I heard footsteps behind. The moon was still bright and unsullied. Not a cloud. There might never have been a raid. Dawn could not be so very far away, but as yet there was no sign.

As the great marble façade of the station loomed up, I bent to tie my shoe. There should have been some subtler way but I had not been taught it. Two men. Not one. Two men followed. This perhaps was the direct result of an unfortunate accident in a Venetian canal. I had thought all along that had been a mistake. Such confidence as had been growing in me hurriedly left by a back door.

The enormous booking hall, usually crowded, was almost deserted. Telephones to the left. Just to cover myself I went to a booking window and asked what was the next train for Venice. Then I stopped to buy a magazine and got a first good

glimpse of the two men buying grapes in cellophane paper
from a girl with a wagon. The light was bright there. Both
young; one tall with a square Teutonic face, fair hair, steel-
blue eyes; the other hook-nosed, thin. Their looks dispersed
the last hopes that they might not belong to the U.A.1
branch of the German Secret Police. Even in Germany, I
think, they would have looked what they were.

Telephone booth. Andrews' number in Venice. A matter
of two or three minutes only. Andrews' soft-spoken accentless
Italian.

"*Pronto, si?*"

"Signor Brevio?"

"*Si, si?*"

"Catania speaking. From Milan."

"Just a minute . . . Yes?"

"An air raid tonight," I said. "The meeting arranged for
tomorrow has been postponed. The principal speaker has
been put out of action."

A longer pause. I had an offensive picture of Jane waking in
the dark beside him, Andrews with a palm over the mouth-
piece saying, keep quiet, it's Mencken.

"Out of action?" Andrews' voice. "Temporarily or permanently?"

"Permanently." I had been thinking how to tell what had
happened without its being understandable to a listener.
"Reich doctor was there and took down what notes he could,
but I arrived too late. This may make a big difference as it
may be that all other notes have been destroyed. Shall I be
seeing you as arranged?"

"Certainly. Follow your instructions."

"I do not think my instructions cover the present situation.
Do you remember that—er—that dealer who went into liquidation only last Monday?"

"Yes?"

"Well, two representatives of the same firm are again in touch with me."

"Oh . . . You're sure it is the same firm?"

"Quite sure."

"Oh . . . Have they attempted to interfere with your normal trading?"

"Not yet. But one has just entered the next telephone box to me now."

"Where are you?"

"Milan station."

"Has your employer arrived yet?"

"No, not yet."

There was a pause.

"Listen, Catania. We are coming to join you today. Until then you must try to do the best you can. If your employer arrives, keep in close contact with him. This will be a protection for yourself. If he does not come, then the initiative as to how you spend the day is very much your own. You won't need me to urge you to avoid any dealings with the representatives of the rival firm."

"I have no wish to go into liquidation," I said dryly.

"Nor do we wish you to. But spend the day as I say. This afternoon—early this evening—go to see our friends, whose address we gave you. We have arranged for you to call, but at a special time only. Not before six o'clock and not after six-thirty. Capito?"

"Capito."

"Between those times arrangements have been made to meet all eventualities. If by then you have been able to disengage yourself from those rival representatives, it will be a very desirable thing. But in any case go."

"I'll go."

In the next box the hook-nosed German was thumbing through the phone book. I could not see the other man.

After I had hung up I telephoned two other numbers at random, from which, not unnaturally at that time of the morning, there was no reply.

I left. In the square outside workmen were waiting for a tram to take them into the center of the city. The sky was bright behind the station, green and gold and blush pink.

The tram came and there was a rush for it. Somehow I got on board, pressed like a sardine. The hook-nosed man was left behind. I got off at the Piazza Cavour. Unfortunately there had been a taxi.

Early breakfast at a small popular café where there were already some customers. Safety in numbers again; and after the nightly raid people wanted extra nourishment before the day began. They needed to talk, to sip a drink and relax. My friend took a table by the door and ordered something in a glass.

The waiter, thin and middle-aged, had a worried, depressed look. He had a brother, he said, making aircraft engines at the Faroni works. One had tried to get through before coming on duty but they said the line was engaged. Why not say "down" and have done with it? The main railway line, one heard, had been hit, five kilometers north of the city. One did not at all know where it was going to end. This bombing of cities was so *barbarous*; it was like sacking a town in the old days; it was a return to Alaric. Things were at a pretty pass.

"Do not worry," I said. "The Germans have done far worse to the British. We must trust in our friends."

He nodded unconvincingly. "Yes, yes, of course. But it is all rather confusing, this war. Not like the last; that was clear-cut eh? Enemies, friends? Does one reverse them at will like a tablecloth? And all in a lifetime, *signore*. I do not know."

Afterward I walked to the Duomo and went inside. Mass was being celebrated in one of the aisles, and on impulse I joined the group praying and took the sacraments. It was the first time for nearly a year, but today it seemed proper, as a man might before battle. In times of danger the old rituals count.

Later I sat in the square in brilliant sunshine and read the *Corriera della Sera.* Censored and regimented by Fascism, the great Liberal newspaper still clung to the dignity of its original outlay as if the façade would deceive people into thinking it could still call its soul its own. Today there was an angry editorial against the "un-neutral" attitude of Greece.

I put a hand up to scratch my chin, and this led me to a barber's shop where I had a shave, a haircut, a shampoo, a manicure. This exhausted my inventiveness, but before it was done a tall blond young man with a square head and blue-gray eyes took a chair beside me. His Italian accent was good but not good enough. He came from Berlin, or even farther east. We ignored each other.

There was a telephone in the shop and I rang the Hotel Colleoni. Yes, there had been a message for me from a Captain Bonini of Venice, cancelling his booking of the two rooms. Would I kindly collect my case when convenient?

Did that mean the conference was altogether cancelled? It might be specially helpful to Andrews if I could find out. Why not go to the Faroni works now?

Observing that the German was still having his hair cut I left the shop rapidly and was lucky enough to see a taxi. I got in and in a moment we were skimming through the streets. A glance through the back window showed no one following. I might just be free, but to be sure I leaned forward and gave the driver instructions to take a roundabout way, choosing his own way through the back streets of the industrial district.

He gave a sidelong stare but did as he was told. When we turned in at the gates of the factory I thought the double maneuver had been successful. There was certainly no car in sight.

The gates were not guarded and we drove on until where the floes of broken glass began.

"Wait here," I said, and crunched across to the houses. Some of the sheds were still smoldering and very little had been done to clean up the debris of the night.

I knocked on the door of the house with drawn blinds, waited, knocked again and then saw the secretary with the bandaged head coming across the garden toward me.

"What can I do for you?"

"You will remember me. Catania of the Admiralty Staff. I have been instructed to call and make one or two inquiries."

He fidgeted with the bandage. "Oh, very well. Come in."

He opened the door and led the way into a room on the right. The sun filtered in through the fine cracks in the venetian blind.

"Ferocchi is my name. I can only give you a few minutes."

"Chiefly I want to know if the conference has been canceled or postponed."

"You should know that. The Admiralty was informed this morning that it was postponed for one week."

I frowned. "I am sorry. I have been out of touch since early this morning. Am I to understand, then, that the results of Professor Brayda's researches are not lost after all?"

Ferocchi hesitated. "So far nothing useful has been found. The laboratory is burned out. But the conference will be held to review other matters. It was not convened solely for one purpose."

"Of course. Of course. Can you tell me whether Dr. von Riehl will attend the conference next week?"

"No. Dr. von Riehl is returning to Germany tomorrow."

"Thank you. I'll not trouble you further. You must be very tired."

"War is a tiring business," said Ferocchi.

I moved to go. "There is one thing: it is a purely personal matter but I could not help noticing and resenting Dr. von Riehl's attitude toward you. He seemed to think you doubted his word."

"Oh, that," Ferocchi closed his eyes. "One becomes used to arrogance . . . But last night—I have worked for Professor Brayda for three years. I am no scientist, but I am convinced he was not talking nonsense after we carried him upstairs."

"Then . . ."

"Oh, who am I to say?" He shrugged. "This is just a personal opinion and I must ask you not to pass it on . . ."

"Of course."

"I do not feel that the Herr Doktor will break his heart if nothing is ever found. In wartime there is patriotism to add to professional jealousy. I think Dr. von Riehl knows what Professor Brayda succeeded in doing, and I think he is taking the knowledge home with him to Germany."

"But Germany is our ally!"

"And how long before she is something more? The Herr Doktor is making sure and putting Germany first."

"If you have been with the professor so much," I said, "even though you are not a scientist, have you not gathered what he hoped to do?"

Ferocchi looked at me suspiciously. "He was working on a blister gas and experimenting with its effect on rats. He was startled and somewhat alarmed by the results. That is all I can tell you."

"Thank you. I gathered that was so from what he said just before he died. I also got the impression that he was not wandering in his mind until immediately before the end."

"He had a very clear mind," said Ferocchi. "It would be the last part to succumb."

I walked back to the taxi and got in.

"Piazza del Duomo," I said. There was no sign of the men who had been following me. I was free again.

Meeting the secretary had been a lucky chance. I had quite a lot to tell Andrews. Perhaps I could tell him and then leave the country. The thought of peaceful work in the, at present, peaceful English countryside was like a healing balm to frayed nerves.

Yet, for a person conditioned all his life to intellectual rather than physical activity, I had not done so badly. Acting on my own initiative here, I had discovered a lot.

I peered out of the back window. A tram car, a donkey cart, a large black limousine. No sign of the other taxi. This part of Milan was unfamiliar. I realized that the driver thought his earlier instructions still applied and was making a devious way back.

I leaned forward. "Go straight back," I said. "Don't bother to drive round."

He half turned his head and nodded. My stomach congealed and became liquid. It was not the same driver.

CHAPTER 12

The difference between cool action in a crisis and losing one's head is surprisingly small.

My first thoughts were: this *is* the other taxi: they're in the limousine: you're alone yet: don't let them know you suspect.

I sat on the edge of the seat and tried to swallow something in my throat as big as a billiard ball. Think. It's your only chance. Think.

Probably an ordinary taxi with an ordinary Italian driver acting on their instructions. Which way going? Toward the sun? South. Must act soon while car still in Milan. But going too fast to jump. Screeching but slowing at corners; broken leg better than capture.

This the long-expected move. The zigzag drive to the Faroni works a bad mistake; it showed I knew they were following me and therefore would not lead them to any other members of my organization. So they'd now try their own means: persuasion by the *tötschlager*. Taxi door opened away from me, hinge at back, so hard to slip out of car. Suburban villas flashing past; a church, trees, a railway bridge. What if I told the man to stop? If he was not one of them he had been heavily bribed.

Car slowing. Nothing on the road ahead. Going to turn. Limousine overtaking. Quite suddenly both cars slithered to a stop abreast of each other. The jerk of the stoppage was so sudden that my hand was flung off the door handle. I grasped it again, but a man had jumped in on the other side: the wide-set eyes; the close cropped head; his revolver had a long metal silencer. "Sit still!"

We screamed into a rocket-like acceleration, leaving the limousine behind. The driver's gears clashed as he would not wait for the change. The street had been empty; no one had seen. "Sit still!" said the man again.

Perhaps that was when I lost my head, but at that moment there seemed only one thing to do. I lurched forward and got my forearm round the driver's throat . . . the German did not fire but quickly reversed his revolver.

We swiveled across the road, missing a van, jolted on the pavement, screamed alongside a wall, metal tearing, swerved away, hit the wall at an angle and crashed through it into a garden, plowed through shrubs and turned over.

Pain was shouting from a split in my head, and my hands were on fire.

I tried to sit up. A lot of confused noise, people talking. My face streaming with blood. Someone had me by the arm.

"He's coming round," said a voice.

"All the same it was a nasty bang," said another. "Some concussion, no doubt. Also the hands. Since the ambulance is on its way for the taxi driver . . ."

"Extremely kind," said a third. "But Signor Catania is a friend of mine. I would not think of letting him go to a hospital when my home is so near." In a lowered voice: "He is, you will understand, on important business for the Admiralty, and we do not wish it known that he is in Milan."

"Of course, in that case . . . If you will wait a few minutes he will be fit to be moved to your car."

"It is hardly necessary to wait. Between us we can carry him a few yards."

"A few minutes rest would be better; but if this is a matter of any urgency . . ."

For a while I had been too dazed to realize what was wrong with this conversation. I now opened my eyes, and knew.

I was still in the garden. The liquid on my face was water not blood. Bending over me were the two Germans, about to pick me up; beyond were two strangers, Italians, one who looked like a professional man. Some others, including a woman, were exclaiming loudly about the overturned car. My sight was black with pain, and I wanted to go to sleep again.

Hands under my armpits. I struggled. "No! . . . I refuse! . . ."

They were carrying me. I kicked.

"Wait," said the doctor. "He may have internal injuries. Put him down a moment."

"It is nothing," said the hook-nosed German impatiently. "Some nervous aftermath of the accident. The sooner he is away from all these people the better. Rest is all he needs."

The doctor ignored this. "Have you any pains in the limbs? Any difficulty breathing?"

"Yes!" I said. "Pain—pain in the chest."

"We will get him the best medical attention," said the tall German. "My own doctor can be with him in twenty minutes. He will be called in any case. I need some attention for bruises myself."

The Italian said to me: "How do you feel now? The hospitals are busy and your friend has offered to drive you to his home. If you will allow these gentlemen to carry you to their car . . ."

Someone was supporting me by the shoulders in a benevolent manner. I struck out with my hand.

"No friend . . ."

"This gentleman, I mean."

I tried to concentrate on the tall man, the butt end of whose Luger had done me more damage than the car accident.

"I have never—seen him before—in my life."

The tall man shrugged. "You see. We were sharing the same taxi, as you know, talking together when it happened. He is still dazed, but he will be quite well after a rest."

The doctor was looking at me thoughtfully. I was conscious of one great asset in this argument: I spoke Italian like an Italian, they did not.

"I would have thought perhaps a few hours observation . . ."

"Hospital," I said. "Yes. Hospital."

Just then there was a stir among the people and I heard the word "*ambulanza.*"

"I insist," said the big German, "that Signor Catania comes with us. As you say, the hospitals are very busy. Besides, it is the secrecy of his business here. I have told you he will be well looked after."

But he had made the mistake of pressing too hard.

"It is at my own discretion," said the doctor. "The responsibility is mine, not yours. His name need not come out. He has expressed a wish to go to hospital—"

"Cer-certainly," I agreed.

"So you see . . . there is no more to be said. But of course you may go with him if you wish."

The tall man was white with annoyance. I thought he almost might pull his gun, but instead he gave a contemptuous shrug and pushed a way out through the gathering crowd, followed by his companion. The relief of seeing them go was like a salve to my splitting head and bleeding hands. There were many worse shifts than spending a few hours in hospital. When the ambulance men came for me I was put on a stretcher and carried to the waiting car. The last I saw of the accident was a view of a broken wall and of a taxi wheel upended to the sky.

They took me to the Ospedale Maggiore. The doctor who examined me there was an efficient and kindly man.

"There is no serious injury that I can find. Your hands are much cut but no veins have been severed. It was one of the side windows of the taxi, I understand. How could this accident ever have happened on a straight road?"

"The car seemed to skid."

"Your head must have been hurt as the car overturned, for the injury is at the back. This too is not serious, but you will need to take things easy for a day or two. I will give you an antitetanus injection and something to soothe your nerves."

"How badly is the driver injured?"

"A broken leg and injuries to the ribs. It will be some days before he will have the pleasure of explaining to the police how it happened. He may well lose his license. Of course with so many in the services, all sorts are permitted to ply for hire."

The doctor shot something into my arm.

"When shall I be able to leave? I have an important appointment this evening."

"We'll see. Is your chest still paining?"

"That's quite gone. I think it was just the shock."

He studied me for a minute. "Don't underrate this accident. Shock can be delayed as well as immediate. Drink this."

I swallowed his bitter draft. The ward was full, for a

number of extra patients had been drafted in here to make room for air-raid casualties.

One of the nuns came by, and the doctor said: "A light meal if he wakes, but I don't think he will. I'll see him again tomorrow morning."

"Was that a sleeping draft?" I asked in sudden alarm.

He nodded. "You are very much on edge. It's a precaution and soothes the nerves. You will sleep for a little while and then be better."

"Sleep how long? I must be awake by five!"

"Naturally, my friend. You'll be awake before then. But be quiet now. I'll be around early in the morning."

I looked after him; he was talking to the nun as they walked away. My watch. It was just noon. I *must* wake at five. My head was heavy but not with the cracking heaviness of half an hour ago. My hands were bandaged and soothed. I *must* wake at five. That seemed a comforting long way off. I began to feel relaxed. For the moment I was safe. My eyelids drooped and I went to sleep.

A nun wheeling a trolley. There were dim lights in the ward, and someone was groaning down at the other end. I was interested in nothing. My eyelids closed again; soft pillows of sleep pressed down. Falling through resilient feathery clouds. What had Andrews said? A ham-tomato omelet. The sirens had gone and I must warn Jane Howard. But if there was an explosion Dr. von Riehl would be left alone to manufacture the improved gas. The bells of the Campanile were only to ring if there was an invasion, if the Germans got across the Channel.

I opened one eye again. What had Andrews said? They were going to operate on Jane Howard for espionage. Silly . . . espionage not a disease. What was it? Andrews kept a shop in Milan. The name was Lorenzo. Not Andrews but Manuel Lorenzo. Not espionage. Lorenzo.

I struggled into a sitting position. "Listen, what time is it?"

The young nun came slowly over. "Lie down and go to sleep: it is quite early yet."

"I must know the time! What is it?"

"About six."

"Six!" I fought against nausea and a bursting head. "I must get up! Where are my clothes?"

She looked alarmed; she was very young. "You must not get up without the permission of a doctor! *Abbiate cura!* you will injure yourself!"

I was out of bed, on my knees, fighting the need to vomit, groping under the bed for a parcel of clothing which might be there.

"Be quiet, can't you?" said the man in the next bed. "My stomach is paining, and I can't get any rest with this going on."

"I'll fetch a doctor," said the nurse, and fled.

I found the parcel, pulled it out, rested my head for a few seconds against the blanket. Thick furry ropes of sickness were pulling at my throat.

"He's delirious!" said the man in the next bed. "They should get someone quickly; he might get violent. I couldn't do anything, not with my stomach."

I sat back on the bed, fumbled with the wrappings of the parcel. It was the effects of the sleeping draft. And the bandages on my hands made every finger a thumb. At last I got the string away: shirt, tie, pants, trousers, everything here, except what had been in the pockets.

The girl was some time in coming back, and by then I had struggled into some of the things. Not a doctor but an older nun with her. I lay back against the bedrail, taking deep breaths.

"What is this? You cannot begin to get up until—"

"Please listen, Sister!" I had been gathering my faculties for this. "Through . . . motor accident this morning I was brought in here. Deeply appreciate your attention and care. But I must leave tonight. Quite essential. I am attached to the Admiralty and have important report to make. This is wartime and . . . this is wartime . . ."

My mind went blank; temporarily I'd lost the crux of the argument.

"The report can be sent," she said. "We can telephone and tell them of your accident."

"That wouldn't do . . . confidential and must not commit it to writing. This is wartime and . . ." The words came, ". . . and *you would not refuse a soldier permission to deliver an important message because of a trifling injury?*"

I saw hesitation in her eyes "You are suffering from concussion. In the doctor's judgment—"

"Quite recovered. The sleeping draft has left me a little heavy in the head, that is all. If you could help me to dress . . . my wallet and watch."

She shrugged her shoulders. "Oh, very well, sir, if you wish it. We must not, as you say, hinder the war. But I think you are unwise. I will see that one of the sisters goes with you."

"Extremely kind." I went on dressing in clumsy haste. If it were already six . . . "I wonder . . . might I have a drink of something?" Nausea returning.

The water revived me, and my watch when it came was another goad. Fifteen minutes past six.

Formalities of departure took too long: forms to sign, records of discharge to file: it must have been six-thirty by the time I stood on the threshold of the hospital looking for a taxi, with a middle-aged nun holding my arm.

Of course there was no taxi and I waited in a fever of impatience. The sun had set by now and the short twilight was rapidly fading. It was no real distance to walk, but I stood there fuming, knowing as every minute ticked away that if a taxi would only come . . .

In the end I could wait no longer. The nun came with me as far as the Via Ospedale, where the traffic was at its busiest; people hurrying home before the difficulties of the blackout; but there, with still no taxi appearing, she hesitated, and I said, no, I would do well enough on my own. I thought I would be slightly less conspicuous, even bandaged as I was, without the company of a nun (everyone stared), and I was unwilling anyhow to let her come the whole way.

But after she had gone I realized that things were still not good. In the Piazza San Stefano all the traffic suddenly blurred, and I leaned against a lamp standard. My head had seemed to open a great mouth at the back and suck in a gust of ice-cold air. I gritted my teeth and waited, barely conscious, until the worst was past.

"You are sick, *signore?*" A man stopped solicitously. "You were hurt in the air raid? Why do you not go into the church and sit down?"

"Nothing," I said. "Slight indisposition. Have you . . . a cigarette?"

He gave me one, and I thanked him and drew at it uncertainly. Others had stopped, and to save a crowd I moved on. At the entrance to the Via Beccaria I stopped, dropped the cigarette, saw it roll across the pavement, wondered if I could bend to pick it up. Darkness was falling.

A car drew up beside me. "Taxi, *signore?*"

At last. Just in time. Even now—

With a hand on the door of the car I stopped. Something had gone wrong the last time I took a taxi. With an effort I remembered what it was.

I withdrew my hand. The taxi appeared to be swaying.

A hand gripped my hand. "Let me help you in."

He was a tall dark man with a fleshy self-confident face. I remembered him as a bystander at the accident.

Something was pressing into my side. As I opened my mouth a hand went over it. At this my knees completely gave way, and my sudden dead weight pulled away from the hands that held me. I collapsed on the pavement and lay full length. A woman saw me and screamed. A man stood over me, but I shouted at the top of my voice. The taxi drew sharply away.

People crowded round. I lay still and gasped and groaned. The man had gone. A policeman was crossing the street.

"A dispute over a taxi," said the woman who had screamed. "I saw them quarreling and this one fell!"

"He is injured! He is dying!"

"What is the matter? Why has the taxi gone?"

I half sat up, and then was helped to my feet. Voices and faces jostled each other.

"It was nothing," I said to the policeman. "As the lady said. A man claimed he had hailed it first. He pushed me and I fell . . . I have been in hospital with air-raid injuries."

There was a murmur of sympathy.

"Where is the man?" said the policeman. "Which way did he go?"

No one knew.

"Perhaps he took the taxi. You had better have another. Do you wish to make a statement?"

"No, no, certainly not. It is quite unimportant."

It took some minutes to find another taxi—they were not really allowed to cruise for fares—and I was helped in, half fainting in the darkness.

"Where do you wish to go?" asked the policeman.

"Lorenzo & Co., Via Monte Rosa, 11."

The door slammed. Gray streets and odd lights flittered

past. If this was the fake taxi then I was done. It might just have driven round a block.

I stared out. Nothing to be seen of the hotels in the Corso Vittorio Emanuele. Trams clanging. It was dark. Sounding of horns. Perhaps this was the end.

But not quite. The taxi stopped and the driver opened the door.

"See here. Lorenzo & Co. That will be eight lire."

I gave him ten before getting out. The street was quieter than expected, but it was the right place. No mistake. There was the name of the shop over the door in gilt letters.

My knees were holding better. I glanced along the way we had come and saw another taxi moving very slowly toward us, practically curb crawling. So they had not lost the scent. I hoped the arrangements to receive me were adequate for this sort of emergency. I hoped, whatever they were, that they did not require *any* more exertion on my part tonight. All I wanted was a drink and to lie down.

My own taxi turned round and made off the way it had come. The other car was still a hundred meters away and still slowly approaching. I turned and walked unsteadily but with confidence up to the door of the shop.

But the shop was shut.

CHAPTER 13

Of all the moments of this nasty day, this was the darkest and bitterest of them all. To reach your promised bolt-hole and to find it closed against you, to be trapped and ill and alone, and darkness falling.

They say the unknown is the worst thing to face; but I would have stood any unknown danger better than this known evil that was coming to me. I knew it all: the cellar and the rubber truncheons and the weakness of the flesh. In that last awful summer in Vienna I had sat behind two storm troopers on a tram and one had complained that his shoulder was stiff. The other said, why? And the first man, with a boyish grin, had answered: I was beating up lousy Jews all night.

Nausea had been assailing me on and off ever since I woke, and now it had its way: I was sick in the corner, in the darkness, like an injured dog. When it was over I fumbled in my pocket and felt with relief the pencil Dwight had given me.

The approaching taxi had stopped about fifty meters away.

The reason was plain: on the other side two women were passing. There must be no observers; the thing must not be bungled again. Two men got out of the taxi.

A last instinct of escape awoke in me again. I backed into the shop porch, pencil still in hand, rattled the handle of the door, beat on the door. An iron grille was down and this rattled and shook. No answer. I jerked and wriggled at the handle. The women were just passing on the other side of the street.

Beside the shop was a narrow alley. I went down it, blindly, not reasoning now. It was a cul-de-sac—at the end a door. It might in some way be connected with the shop. As I hammered on it two figures appeared at the mouth of the alley. They must have sprinted, thinking I might get away. Now, seeing me trapped, they stopped, waiting for the taxi to come up.

I thumped and hammered again, hurting my injured fist, pencil raised to mouth.

The door opened. In the darkness a shriveled old woman peered angrily up at me.

"How dare you make such a noise! What do you want?"

I half stumbled, pushing at the door, but she held it firm.

"Lorenzo & Co.!"

"They are shut." She was stronger than I was and the gap was narrowing.

"Manuel Lorenzo!" I said choking. "I wish to see him!"

"Come round in the morning. We open at eight."

"Tomorrow will not do! I must see him tonight!"

"You cannot see him . . . Wait. I will ask."

"Let me in!" I said. "I am not well: I am going to faint."

"It's after shop hours. We don't admit people after—"

Footsteps behind me: I pushed again and this time I was stronger or she weaker, for I forced a clumsy way in, past the old woman who was proclaiming shrilly, stumbled in a dark passage against a bicycle, caught on to a shelf to save the fall.

Heard the door shut behind me. Really shut. For a moment a breathing space.

I stuffed the pencil away. "*Signora*, I implore you—"

"Be quiet," she said. "Can you walk?"

A complete change in her voice. "A little way. You see—"

"Follow me, then. But have a care for our stock."

She led the way to the end of the passage and up stairs. I made these noisily, kicking against the steps. At the top she said: "Hush, be quiet," and led me across a wide showroom full of dummies and rolls of cloth. Twice she had to stop for me, because only a tiny pilot light burned.

We went into a lighted office with a roll-top desk and a safe. Two men were counting money. The old woman said something I could not catch and I sat heavily in a chair.

"I told you he was not to be let in!" one of the men said harshly.

"I know. *I know*. I gave all possible hints. But look at him? *In extremis*. What could I do!"

The man came across. He was small, middle-aged, with cheeks like canyons.

"Manuel Lorenzo," I said with difficulty, repeating my lesson. "Via Monte Rosa, 11. I wish to see him."

"I'm afraid we cannot oblige, *signore*. You should have gone to the Monumental Cemetery."

"The—"

"Manuel Lorenzo has been dead ten years. Perhaps, as his son, I can oblige."

"But I was . . ."

"How did you come by that injury?"

It was past time to consider whether anything would be lost by telling the truth. "The German secret police tried to kidnap me. I escaped with the injuries you see. I only left hospital at six-thirty."

"So that was why you were so late for your appointment. It has made things very difficult for us."

The other man came across carrying a glass. He was younger, with spectacles, close cropped fair curly hair. "Drink this."

Cognac. I had wanted water but the cognac went down, burning all the way.

"Manuel Lorenzo," I said.

"Forget about him. Tell us what happened."

I tried to. I gained strength as the words strung themselves together.

When it was over the elder man rubbed a furrow in his cheek. "It will be very dangerous now, Ricci. Are you still willing to try?"

"Of course. It may divert suspicion from us."

"Not if you put bandages about your head and your hands."

"The diversion will make it easier for you to get him out of the house."

"I cannot take him now. Maria will have to go."

"Well, it will be easier for her, then."

"Oh, have it your own way. But we can't help you if you run into trouble."

The fair-haired man turned to me. "How long before you feel able to walk?"

"I can move now."

"Come with me, then."

I pushed myself up from the chair and moved toward a door he held open. Within was a small fitting-room with mirrors.

"I want your hat and your suit and your tie," said Ricci, "I'll fetch you a new suit to wear."

I was to have come to the shop and asked for Manuel Lorenzo, a sufficient guide to my identity. I was to have been taken to the tailoring department and fitted for a ready-made suit. In fifteen minutes a man dressed in my clothes would walk out and leave the shop. Anyone waiting would recognize the superficial likeness and follow. In the meantime I would have left by another entrance in a new suit.

"But why," I asked, "was this only to be effective during the last half-hour of business? Why could I not have come earlier in the day?"

"Because after six the light begins to fail. If this were done in bright day the deception would be likely to be seen."

The scheme had a touch of brilliance because it could all have happened without incriminating anyone in the shop. Now everything had gone awry. I had come after closing time and hammered on a side door. The man who took my place was clearly acting as a decoy and was in much greater danger; and Lorenzo & Co. were incriminated.

"This is not good," I muttered, as I watched Ricci go. "He is simply taking over the risks I ran."

Signor Lorenzo shrugged. "Ricci is a fit man and you are not. He will not be knocked on the head at the first corner. So long as the deception is not immediately seen through. Are you ready to go?"

I had two more gulps of cognac and put the half empty flask in my pocket. The old woman was tying a scarf over her gray head.

"I must sincerely thank you for this," I began to Lorenzo. "If—"

"We do not do it for thanks," was the dry answer.

"I am waiting," said Maria from the door.

I followed her downstairs to the door by which I had entered, then down again. She had a torch, and we picked our way through two cellars stocked with piece-goods. In the second cellar was a large cupboard. We entered this, and as she shut the door the back of the cupboard opened and we

stepped out into another cellar. Through this and up a flight.
Head throbbing again.

A door. "Careful now," she said.

Another alley. She peered out, her breath coming quickly
like a fox. It was dark.

I followed her through the door, and we hurried down the
alley keeping close to the wall; came to a cross-way and took
the left turn.

She touched my arm. "You would draw attention in a
tram. We will go by taxi from the end here. There is a rank
on the corner. Say to the driver Santa Maria della Grazie."

We came out on a busy street. Three taxis. We chose the
middle one, and in a moment I was sitting back, the curt old
woman at my side. The relief threatened to bring back weakness again. As the taxi crawled through the center of the city
I recognized the turn down the Via Meravigli, and in a few
minutes I was paying off the man outside the fine old Bra-
mante Church where da Vinci painted his great fresco.

Before the car had started again the old woman was pulling
at my arm. I stopped for a gulp of cognac and then went with
her through two or three poor streets until we reached the
back entrance of a warehouse. She took out a key and un-
locked a wicket door. We went up steps.

"Ricci," I said, breaking a long silence between us. "I
should wish to know that he comes to no harm. Perhaps you
will be able to send word."

We went through another storeroom. Her torch showed up
the name *Lorenzo* on one bale.

"We do not send word in this business," she said. "If you
wish to know anything ask the people in here. I must get
back."

She had knocked at a door. A tall man opened it. Major
Dwight.

CHAPTER 14

It would be an understatement to say I was relieved to see him. I had been too long on my own, making decisions in a vacuum, struggling just to stay alive. It seemed like a month, not two days.

He was alone in a little office place, not unlike the one I had just left. I collapsed in a swivel chair, while the old woman went into voluble explanations. When she had done she hitched her shabby black knitted cardigan round herself and left.

Dwight bit at his pipe with long yellow teeth and looked me over impersonally, like a vet with a sick horse on his hands.

"Groggy?"

"Not bad."

"Dead beat?"

"More or less."

He put a hand on my arm. "Come along. I'll show you what you need, old man."

He led me into a bare little room with a radio set, a divan bed, some photographic negatives curling in a washbasin. He pointed to the bed.

"Get undressed and put out the light. A spot of shut-eye. I'll give you three hours. We'll have a full powwow then."

"I could do with a drink—just cold water, if you have it."

"The tap's there. Entirely *potabile*. I'll wake you at 10:30."

I had craved sleep so much while fighting off the effects of the sedative that now perversely it seemed far away. Nerves were too much on edge . . .

He was shaking my arm and telling me it was nearly eleven.

I dressed again, still shaky; sluiced face and hands, and the sting of the cuts seemed to revive me. I drank another glass of water and went into the office, to find them *all* there.

Quite a reunion. Andrews, apparently feeling the heat, had flung off his coat and wore a *setta pura* emerald green shirt with a long loose tie showing green gondolas on a red background. A broad gray velour belt kept his striped trousers up.

And Jane . . . well, I did not take in all that about Jane except that she was here. My face had, I think, flushed on seeing her, and the expression in her eyes startled me and lit up my mind.

Now I told them everything that had happened, and was glad Dwight had insisted on the extra rest before hearing me. When I had done they asked endless questions, chiefly Dwight walking up and down and swearing quietly from time to time under his breath. Andrews sat quietly twine-toed biting at his thumbnail.

"It means," said Dwight, "the complete destruction of our system in Milan. Damned bad luck, old man; it wasn't your fault, but there it is. It means the virtual break-up of Lorenzo & Co. unless—"

"I'm *sorry*," I said.

"Unless," said Jane, "these men don't tell the Italian O.V.R.A. about Lorenzo."

"We couldn't risk it."

"They've acted on their own so far."

"Luckily for Mencken, otherwise he would hardly have stood a chance."

"Robert's hands ought to be seen to," Jane said. "They're bleeding."

I looked down. "It's nothing. I took the bandages off to wash." I was feeling better at last.

"I'll get them and put them on again," she said.

There was silence while she was out of the room. Andrews was whistling lightly between his teeth. She came back and began to bandage my hands.

Dwight said: "I doubted all along if the gallop was going to be worth while. We've sacrificed one of our best bloody systems for absolutely nothing."

"What about Ricci?" I said.

"He came to no harm."

"That at least I am thankful for."

"No harm so far, at least. One doesn't know where the ramifications are going to end."

"Some of these cuts are quite deep," Jane said. Her hands were cool and slightly caressing.

Andrews twisted a lighted match so viciously that it hummed as it flew out of the window.

"We do not know yet if we have sacrificed one of our best systems for *absolutely* nothing. This is what Dr. Mencken has yet to tell us. Will you explain, Mencken, please, a little more of what you learned of Professor Brayda's work and why you think as you do about von Riehl."

I tried to. When I had finished Dwight said: "I think he's right. Dorio, who is keeping tag on von Riehl, said he had made arrangements to stay in Milan for five days—with an occasional trip to Garda no doubt thrown in. Now he's canceled his arrangements here and has wired Fräulein Volkmann to tell her of the change."

"Who is Fräulein Volkmann?" I asked.

"His Strength through Joy," said Dwight. "You know, old man."

Andrews got up and hitched his trousers over his stomach. "You got a pretty good idea, from what Brayda said in your presence, what he had been working on?"

"Oh, yes."

"A new gas?"

"Not new," I said. "But a rather startling development of an old. He is using chlorovinyl di-chlorarsine as a starting point. He also frequently mentioned bromo-benzylcyanide, but I was not able to follow whether this was to be developed as an alternative or whether some amalgamation was in his mind. The first result of the improvement, so far as I could make out, would be to have an effect similar to chlorovinyl di-chlorarsine but with a much heightened persistency figure."

"Very fascinating," said Andrews. "What does it all mean?"

Jane took my other hand.

"Chlorovinyl di-chlorarsine is a vesicant," I said. "Somewhat like mustard gas, you understand. These gases are the most useful in modern warfare because of their persistency. That is, they can linger two or three weeks in favorable conditions."

"And this improvement?"

"I gather he claimed the increased persistency might leave the components active for months. It would make decontamination very difficult."

Dwight began to cough. Perhaps talking of it had nudged his body's memory.

"But I never gathered whether this persistency would be constant in all conditions. It might—I would guess—be most useful in the summer months when high temperatures are likely."

"This chloro stuff," said Dwight gasping. "Do we know about it?"

"Yes, the British invented it."

He drew back his lips. "What sort of military potential would this improvement have?"

"In actual battle, do you mean? It would depend on the tactics. I suppose for shelling or bombing rear bases it would have great advantages, but for use in a—in what you would call a mobile war, I would think it might defeat its own object by making a place as untenable for an advancing army as for a retreating one."

Andrews laughed sardonically.

"This question of military potential is a hangover from Dwight's last war training, Mencken. Forget about battles. In total war the gun that blows up a pillbox is much less important than the man who spreads dirty stories about the commandant's champagne orgies. So with gas. What I want to know is its effect if dropped on a city—what effect would it have on the morale of the people living there?"

"Well, you cannot live and work in gas masks and special protective clothing for weeks on end. It might, if used in sufficient quantity, make a town quite uninhabitable. But there is one other effect that would have a much more dangerous influence on civilian morale. It was this side-effect that I understood was worrying Brayda . . ."

"Well?"

"He had been experimenting on mice and rats, you know. He found the blisters caused by this gas had a tendency to recur even after months."

"You mean they wouldn't heal?"

"They would heal but then break out again in the surrounding tissues. They tend to ulcerate and become fatal."

There was a silence.

"The blisters would become cancerous?" Andrews asked.

"I am not a medical man. But an ulcer which will not heal might be called that. At least it could very easily give rise to such a belief in a population subjected to it."

"My God!" said Dwight. "That's pretty. That's really pretty." I had never seen such an expression on his face before.

"That is the extent of your information?" Andrews said.

"Yes."

"Well, it's enough. Perhaps our system has not been broken up in vain."

"What can we *do?*" asked Jane.

Andrews got up. "I think we have to assume that von Riehl has enough information—or believes he has enough—to carry back to Germany. Right? Was Dorio able to make a copy of the telegram von Riehl sent to his Fräulein?"

Dwight looked up. "Eh?"

When the question was repeated: "I'll get it." He went out.

Jane had finished my hands. "Thank you," I said.

Andrews rubbed his chin. You could hear the scrape of his thumb.

Dwight came back. "Fräulein Volkmann, Hotel du Lac, Garda. Am unable return Garda. Urgent business cuts our holiday short. Meet me Milan station tomorrow evening to leave by seventeen-fifty train for home. A.R."

Andrews took the copy and read it himself to make sure. Then his eyes went from one to another of us. "Well, that is the position. Any suggestions?"

No one spoke. Dwight passed a hand over his hair. His face had not lost its unpleasant expression.

"There's one solution," he said.

Andrews grunted. "I'm glad you feel that way too."

"We should have to check our facts very carefully," Dwight said, as if he had not wanted to commit himself to a decision and was annoyed at having been forced to do so. "We've got to check on the total destruction of the laboratory—"

"I can vouch for that," I said. "It was a smoldering ruin."

He frowned. "—and check on whether any duplicate notes have been found. It may be impossible to be sure, but we have sources. In the next few hours we've got to squeeze our sources till they squeak. It would be crazy to take on a job like this unless we were certain not only that it was imperative but that it would achieve its object if successful."

"Job?" I said. "What job?"

Andrews sat perfectly still with his fat shoulders slightly hunched like a plump green parrot on its perch.

"On the lowest level, Dwight. On the lowest level it might be worth doing anyway."

"I wouldn't consider moving on the lowest level at all," said Dwight. "There's only one motive would justify it."

"You know what the last report said."

"What last report?" I asked in exasperation.

Jane said: "Reports are issued sometimes, summing up the political aspects of the war. They come from various sources, but they're usually reliable. Aren't they, Vernon?"

"To hell with the last report," said Dwight vigorously. "We've got to check on the destruction of the laboratory and whether other people know what von Riehl knows This is the absolute minimum, before I'm prepared to move at all."

They seemed to be talking in riddles, or as if there was some empathy between them that I could not share. I glanced at Jane, and thought from her expression that somehow she had followed their reasoning part way.

"What do you figure on doing?" she asked.

Dwight said: "You'll not be in this hunt, Jane—nor Mencken. You've both done your part. This is between Andrews and me."

"But what can you *do*? How can you do it?"

"Lay off. You'll get your instructions, such as they are."

I had been thinking. "You mean in some way you are going to try to destroy the information von Riehl carries?"

Andrews laughed. "Trust our half-German friend to put it in such polite language."

I was so angry that for a minute I could not speak. I watched him lighting one of his endless cheroots; his big fleshy face appeared and disappeared through the smoke like that of a djinn in a fairy tale. He seemed to be all grease and discoloration and pitted skin.

"Old man," said Dwight putting his hand on my shoulder and gripping it tight. "Old man, the solution is all too obvious—that's what Andrews means. The difficulty is to face the solution—that's all."

"What *did* the last report say?" Jane asked.

"I've told you, that can't be decisive."

"But it might help us to know. It can't matter now if we all know, can it?"

Dwight hesitated. "Italy is shortly going to move in the Balkans, probably against Greece—as a prestige action, justifying her partnership in the Axis. And she may move east too, from Cyrenaica toward Egypt, at the same time. God help her if she does, I say; but that's not the point. By the end of this month Britain will have five more divisions in the Middle East. We're still desperately short of armor, and might even be called on to help Greece. Our instructions—I mean our personal instructions here—naturally cover any action which might cause disorganization or delay in Italy's war machine. . . . Well, as you know, von Riehl has been in Italy two weeks preparing a report on her supply position. Her supply and production rates are anything but good, and they must be improved. Well, I suppose if anything were to happen to von Riehl and his report were to be destroyed, that of itself would be as potent a single act of disorganization as could be accomplished. That's what Andrews is arguing—that you can justify a killing on two grounds."

So now it was out.

As a man unused to the imperatives of espionage, I was separate from them at this moment—separated even from Jane, though I did not suppose that this had ever happened before in her life.

After what seemed a long time I said: "When does killing cease to be murder?"

Andrews smiled. "When war is declared."

I watched Jane lighting a cigarette from the stub of an old one. I stared at a flying beetle that had come in through the open window and was banging against the light shade. I stared at my neatly bandaged hands.

"It is impossible."

"On what grounds?" Andrews asked evenly. "Morally or literally impossible?"

"Literally anyway," I said with sudden relief. "It could not be done. There is no way to do it."

"There might be."

"Then there is no one—on our side—who *would* do it."

"You've worked in a laboratory, Mencken?"

I stared. "Most of my life."

"The routine work, the small jobs, the checking and filing of details; you might leave such work to your assistants?"

"If I had them, yes."

"And the dangerous experiment, the crucial trial of a theory; to whom would you leave that?"

"I should do it . . ." I stopped before the word "myself."

"I," said Andrews, "have long held a theory which has been held up for lack of the materials to experiment. My theory is that highly-placed Nazis are as mortal as other men. There is a strong feeling in some quarters to the contrary; you may have noticed that few of them develop the diseases ordinary men die of. I shall be interested to put my theory to the test."

"Our orders visualized nothing like this," Dwight said bitterly.

I thought he was prepared to go through with this thing, but unlike Andrews he could not rationalize it, make it a part of his own self-approval.

"Our orders are capable of wide interpretation."

"Not this wide. Von Riehl is a prominent man. What we do is bound to be misunderstood."

"No secret service man ever has the approval of his government. You ought to know that."

Dwight shook his head obstinately. "I wish there wasn't this second reason for acting. That's the only one—if any—that'll get to the world."

"Well, what of it?"

"Our only *real* reason for acting is our belief that von Riehl has knowledge about a poison gas that might otherwise have died with its inventor. If it were not for that we should never have thought of taking any action at all!"

"That's reason enough."

"Of course that's reason enough! But it should be the *only* one! If it comes out, as it will, as a political murder, it may set a fuse for a whole train of assassinations and counterassassinations."

"D'you think I care?" said Andrews, opening his eyes wide. "D'you think I care? This Queensberry Rule stuff makes me want to throw up. The age of chivalry died two hundred years ago, old man. Ask the refugees being machine-gunned and dive-bombed on the roads. Ask them in Rotterdam! Ask them in Prague! Ask them in Warsaw! Grow up, Dwight! Grow up!"

Dwight knocked his pipe out on the windowsill. His face for a moment was completely still, without expression.

"What does Mencken *really* think?" he asked. "He has a pacifist upbringing, but his father died in a concentration camp. What do you feel, Mencken? From what you say, would you entirely oppose it?"

It was an unfair question, to which I had already given a half answer. I glanced at Jane who was smoking furiously. The room was blue with smoke. Of course in my mind I knew this question was a hypothetical one: they would go ahead whatever I said. But what I said mattered something to two of them. And it mattered to me. I was on the brink of a change. Andrews was looking at me quizzically as if he enjoyed my discomfiture.

I said: "On principle I *must* oppose it. By doing this—even by trying to do it—you are proving the true corrosiveness, the true destructiveness of war."

"Why?" said Dwight.

"To destroy a poisonous snake, do you have to become a poisonous snake? This is the crux—the moral crux of the whole thing."

"But to preserve civilization, dear Doctor," Andrews said, "a poisonous snake has to be destroyed."

"Yes, but in a civilized way, otherwise there is nothing left to preserve."

"If Hitler were in this room and you could kill him, would you let him go?"

My father, they said, had died of appendicitis.

"No."

Dwight turned from the window and put his pipe in his pocket.

"We'll break now. You'll be called in the morning."

CHAPTER 15

I dozed fitfully and fretfully through the night, pursued by the shadows of monstrous moral choices. I was wakened at five. Jane too had been trying to sleep but the other two had been out and about all the time.

"We now know mostly what we want to know," Andrews said, almost before we had collected our thoughts. "Last evening Ferocchi, Brayda's secretary, publicly accused von Riehl of withholding information Brayda had passed on to him. Ferocchi was arrested for 'insulting the representative of a brother nation in arms,' but I guess the Italians are upset all the same. At any rate, I think this gives us good enough reason to suppose that Brayda's secret is lost to them. At present *they* certainly suppose it. Now von Riehl sent a code telegram to Berlin yesterday morning. I don't know what was in it; but he isn't likely to have given away enough to deprive himself of the kudos of a personal triumph when he arrives. And the industrial report is going along with him. Incidentally,

according to one of our agents, von Riehl is going to recommend that Nazi *gauleiters* shall be put in charge of all the
principal North Italian factories."

Jane said: "But that's practically taking them over!"

"It won't be represented as that, but it will be the first step.
. . . To continue, we find that von Riehl is spending tonight
at the Hotel Bologna with his two secretaries in attendance.
Tomorrow he is being entertained to lunch at the Palazzo
Reale by the Fascist Council in Milan. They will find good
food for that, no doubt. Tomorrow evening, as we know, he
will leave for Germany in a first-class reserved carriage, but
it will not be a sleeper. It is probable that he intends to work
through the night. He will travel as he came, privately, via
Lucerne, Basle, Frankfurt—"

"Through Switzerland?" I said in surprise.

"Nearly all passenger traffic goes that way," Dwight said,
his legs astraddle a bentwood chair. "It saves worse congestion
on the Brenner line." He began to cough.

"Well?" Jane said.

"Well," said Andrews. "From now until he boards the train
von Riehl will be surrounded by people or at public functions.
But from the time the train leaves Milan he'll be relatively
isolated. It won't be easy even then, because there'll be the
two secretaries, and one of them is an armed S.S. guard. But
he travels all night, and there's two hundred miles of Swiss
territory to cover. Dwight and I are going to catch that
train."

In the silence Dwight's rupturing cough echoed round the
little office. Listening to Andrews, I sometimes wondered if
there were the seeds of a dictator within himself and that it
was this which made him hate the successful dictators so
much.

"What of Fräulein Volkmann?" Jane asked. "She'll be on
the train, won't she?"

"That," said Dwight between his coughs, "is where you come in."

"We have our prejudices," Andrews said. "Even I have my prejudices, and one of them is against making war on women. Particularly as this one would be very likely to get in the way anyhow. I want you to leave for Garda early this morning, Jane. I want you to see that the Volkmann woman stays in Garda long enough for her to miss the Milan express for Basle."

Jane lit another cigarette. "Suggestions?"

"We have none, my dear. You'll have to play it as it comes. Take Mencken with you. Two might contrive it better than one."

I could hardly believe my luck or that Andrews should so order it. I had been expecting every moment to be instructed back to Venice or to resume contact with Captain Bonini.

I do not know if Andrews read my expression but he said to me: "It'll do you no harm to lie low for a day or so. But whatever you do at Garda, be inconspicuous. I'd send you off home right away, but it's only sense to wait until this—mission is decided. It's no good letting you go and then needing you again." He turned. "I rely on you, Jane, to see that he carries out orders."

"Very well," she said, and I thought she colored.

Dwight had at last succeeded in stifling his cough. "It would be best if Mencken's papers were changed now. It's pretty important that his private pack of Gestapo hounds don't pick up his scent again."

Andrews nodded. ". . . A second identity was planned for you, Mencken, in case the first became too hot. Well, it has become too hot. Signor Catania, if he ever reappeared, would be in for trouble. Jane, pass me the blue file on the top of the desk behind you."

She did so. He said: "Everything's here except the passport

photograph. Dwight will take that when you're all fixed up. I don't know what your memory's like, but you should spend the next hour reading this up. All the extra notes we've supplied have to be destroyed before you leave this warehouse."

He handed me the file.

I learned that I was a Yugoslav citizen of Croat descent, born in Zagreb, March 4, 1899. My name was Peter Lansdorf. My eyes were gray, my hair dark brown, graying. I was still five feet ten inches in height, but I lived in Ljubljana and my profession was that of a timber merchant. I had been to Italy to confer with importers in Turin who, under orders, had turned over all their stock to the government and were pressing for a big increase in the export of oak wood from Yugoslavia. What I was doing spending a couple of nights in Garda was not clear, since the papers had not been prepared for this event.

. . . Nevertheless Peter Lansdorf caught the 7:20 A.M. train for Garda that sparkling October morning. His resemblance to Edmondo Catania would not have excited comment. His hair was the same color but worn shorter; he was gray at the temples and round the back of the neck. He wore spectacles which inclined inward to give his eyes a look of being close-set. He evidently felt the nip in the morning air, for he wore a dark coat that was six inches too long. His hat was turned down and a size too large, to accommodate some sticking plaster, and he wore thick woolen gloves.

Though we traveled on the same train I did not sit with Jane on the journey. Orders were orders. At Garda I booked a room in a hotel overlooking the lake, and met Jane about eleven-thirty at a café just north of the walled village.

Hours of valuable discussion time had been lost while we crossed the plains of Lombardy. My own brain had dragged the net for ideas and drawn blank.

When Jane sat down at my table I ordered ersatz coffee and

waited, knowing she had not been idle since she came, but savoring chiefly at this moment the pleasure of being alone with her again.

"Fräulein Volkmann," she said, "leaves at two o'clock from the hotel. She's motoring into Verona because the Venice-Milan express doesn't stop at Peschiera. It reaches Verona at three and is due in Milan at five-thirty."

"And the Basle express leaves Milan at what time: five-fifty? That gives her twenty minutes to change trains. Are they both from the same station?"

"Yes."

I said: "If she were to miss the express at Verona there would be no chance of her catching the one for Basle."

"Oh, no. If she misses it. But how is she to miss it?"

"There's the car journey to Verona."

"I know."

"You have some idea?" I said.

"What makes you think that?"

"The expression in your eyes."

She smiled. "So easy to read?"

"Only in that. Not in anything else at all."

". . . I have an idea. But one would have to be sure it would work."

"What is it?"

"Tell me your ideas first."

"I think I have no aptitude for this sort of thing. I did consider a bogus telegram making other arrangements, but . . ."

"It has the disadvantage that Fräulein Volkmann might telephone to check or ask why. If some suspicion were roused in his mind he might change his plans and that would upset everything."

I looked at my watch. "There's no more than two hours to go. They have given us a tall order."

"Yes. It's the most I've had to do. I'm flattered—and stimulated . . ."

I had not seen it at all that way. "Is it a hired car she is using?"

"That was the one thing I couldn't find out. It looks as if someone she is friendly with at the hotel is driving her. Probably some official if he has gas to spare."

"If we found the car and tampered with the tank. . . . Lack of petrol . . ."

"I guess that would be all right on a deserted road. But the road to Verona is busy. She'd be picked up and catch the train just the same. Anyway, if they leave at two they'll have an hour to cover twenty miles."

I watched her for a moment. My personal feelings were all the time breaking in on the dark business of the day. She had her idea but was deliberately holding it back for her own pleasure. It was like a guessing game; and just now and then one could ignore the grimness of the objective.

I said: "An accident?"

"It might work . . . But it would be difficult to do enough without doing too much, wouldn't it? If she wasn't injured she could still get a lift. And part of the purpose of this is that we're not trying to kill her."

"I give in," I said. "Tell me."

"What we want is something that'll look like a natural mishap—no contrivance about it."

I smiled at her and she smiled back. "I give in," I said again.

She was suddenly mischievous. "Well, I guess it seems to me that instead of delaying the car it would be easier to delay the train."

A peaceful oasis of two hours in all the stress and the danger. A remarkable two hours. It is, I suppose, one of the rewards of the man who lives dangerously: his days are flood-lit in this artificial light of impermanence; the present becomes everything and the future nothing.

I shall always associate that short time with apricots. We had apricot jam with our rolls and coffee, and there was some fragrant climbing plant round the pillars of the café garden which gave off a sweet, warm apricot smell.

The day was brilliant now. When we had reached Peschiera the lake was still shrouded in haze, and only the peaks of the distant Dolomites showed here and there, looking much less substantial than the mountains of cloud. But now it had cleared, and the foothills at the opposite side of the lake looked as if they had been painted there by Tintoretto.

There was much to discuss in Jane's scheme, but once we had talked it out, then it was natural to let it drop—as something decided for better or worse—and turn to ourselves. Almost everything that passed between us I remember, word for word, because in loneliness I have gone over it so often since.

We talked of hills and lakes, of Austria and England and Italy and Australia. She told me more of her married life, which, after the quarrel and the break away in Paris, had settled into a cool, tolerant friendship.

"Maybe we should never have married," she said; "maybe it's a good argument for free love: we should have been lovers for a few months and then parted. But we—took to each other; he seemed to have such charm, to know so much; I was twenty-one, impressionable maybe; we married. There's nothing wrong with him: I don't think there's anything wrong with me. There was nobody else involved either way. It just didn't work out. So we live together now for the convenience of war, and go our separate ways."

"And your separate way leads you into great danger."

She shrugged. "Just being alive is dangerous."

I wanted to speak about Andrews but did not know how.

"You're in it all too deep," I said. "I wish you would leave this task to me this afternoon."

She played a little tune with her fingers on the tablecloth. "I obey orders."

"Andrews should never have given them."

"You don't like Andrews much, do you."

So it was coming. "No. How can I?"

"Why not? He's brilliant at his job."

"I wish—" I said.

"What do you wish?"

"It is not my business. I have no right."

"Robert, what's the matter with you?"

"I wish you weren't involved with him."

"But why me? We all are. We all take orders from him."

I said: "What upsets me is that you take more than orders . . ."

She stared at me. "More than orders? . . ."

"Of course. Do you think I can forget how we met?"

Her eyes widened. "How we . . . But you don't mean . . ."

She broke off again and her hostile expression changed and she began to laugh. She laughed and the waiters turned and looked at her. I had never heard her laugh like this before, and it was a lovely sound; but I hated it because it was directed at me.

"Jane!"

"Oh, Robert . . ." She put her head on my arm. "Sorry. Sorry. It's all Vernon's fault. I thought he'd obviously explain. Isn't that just too bad! I surely beg your pardon . . ." She had stopped laughing but was out of breath. I might have got up in annoyance but her hand was on mine.

"Sorry, Robert . . . one or two other things you've said— I'm sorry to have been so dull."

"*I'm* sorry to have been so dull," I said stiffly, my feelings in a melting pot.

"No, no, no. Do let me *explain*." She swallowed, but did not move her hand away. "He ought to have . . . look, it's like this. Paul is well-off; I buy a lot of clothes; in fact I'm extravagant. I buy them mostly from Lorenzo & Co. of Milan. Every now and again I go to Milan for a fitting. Sometimes too they send me models on approval. Well, some of the models I get have embroidery worked on the neck or the shoulder, or a flower design at the waist; something like that. When they have, I put them on and walk over to Vernon's flat. Then I sit and wait while he spells out the code message which has been embroidered on the frock. That's how we usually get the figures of the Italian output of aircraft. That's how we first received news of the conference . . ."

I stared blankly out at the ultramarine blue of the lake, at the startling purple hills. I stared out at a barge moving down the lake, its red sail extended by the gentle morning *sover*. Sails again now, one of the advantages of the petrol shortage. I looked at the bent old man brushing up the leaves in the roadway. I looked at the row of tall poplars standing like paint brushes against the improbable sky.

Although great pleasure and relief were not far away, I still felt a fool. And although I wanted to believe, some preverse streak in my nature demanded proof. Yet the slightest hint of doubt on my part . . .

"Andrews is fond of women," she said. "Oh, I'll grant you that. But you ought to know he'd never mix business with pleasure."

I said: "Yes."

"Anyway," she said, "I don't think I'm very much flattered with your opinion of my taste in men."

I got up. "I'm *sorry*. You have to see . . ."

"Of course I see," she said. "It was natural. But please sit

159

down. Time's passing so quickly. Too quickly for a mis-understanding . . ."

I sat down and looked at her. She looked at me.

"One last thing," I said. "What did Andrews mean this morning, telling you to see I obeyed orders?"

"Just that. He's not blind, Robert. Or, as it happens, jealous. He just wanted to make sure you and I didn't mix business with pleasure."

The waiter, who had been getting restive at the length of time his customers were staying, came forward to ask if there was anything more. Without consulting Jane I ordered lunch for two, although we had only recently finished breakfast. It didn't seem to matter. We sat in silence until the hors d'oeuvres came. In some way we managed to eat them, still in silence.

"I can't manage a thing more," said Jane, pushing away her plate.

"It's better to try. We don't know when we shall get our next meal."

"We?"

"We."

"That's not obeying orders."

"Damn the orders!"

She made a face, half a wry smile. "It's just what Vernon was afraid of."

I said: "No, it's not. That's not what he was afraid of."

"You're very sure."

"Suddenly on this, yes."

"Why?"

"Jane, you cannot go on with the life you're leading. Not after this business is over. The Lorenzo thing is finished—Andrews said so. Come back to England with me. Your husband can hardly put up any fight about it, if he is as you say. There's still some chance of happiness there."

"Not much while it's being bombed."

"Oddly enough, there is. You are in the front line there, but it is the right side of the line. A man and a woman can make their own lives."

"I don't know. I don't think I could make my own—especially if I'd given this up."

"You could work. There's plenty of honest work in England today."

"It's all very well for you, Robert. You're a chemist of great repute and there aren't many like you. But there are thousands of women who can make munitions. I happen to be the only one who can do this, because of my marriage. If I left I should leave a gap."

The waiter brought the next course and the delicate lake trout tempted our disturbed appetites.

"I'm not a quitter," she said. "After the war. Oh, after the war, my dear . . . Paul wouldn't stand in my way. I'm young. I'll keep . . ."

By right the sun should have gloomed over, but it still shone as brilliantly.

"Youth's a stuff will not endure."

"My own father," she said, "died when he was twenty-eight. Four years older than I am now. His youth didn't endure. I kind of feel that even if two generations are spoiled, we've got to make it right for the next one." She put down her fork. "Sorry to sound like a ghastly propaganda leaflet. I didn't at all mean to."

"The war might go on for years."

"It won't. Not in this country at least. The Italians aren't prepared to face a long war any more than the French were. And other things might happen. America might come in. Then I should *have* to leave."

Her attempt to reassure me was a failure. I waved away the waiter who was bringing a dish of pasta. "What I find impossible is the idea of our parting now, in half an hour. Even if everything goes well, we shall be separating almost at once, for months, probably for years. That is the unbearable thing. Intolerable."

"Would anything at all, make it tolerable?"

"No," I answered. And then quickly: "What do you mean?"

She screwed out her cigarette in the ash tray and went on screwing it round and round long after the last trace of smoke had disappeared.

"After doing this job," she said, "I should catch this evening train back to Venice. I've an excuse for two days' absence from Venice. But my two days won't be up until tomorrow. I could return to Garda, perhaps even stay on."

The vessel with the red sails was almost out of sight round the headland. The stirring breeze raised the scent of apricot. Apricot and warm sunshine and a blue lake.

She said: "If you like, forget I spoke."

"I don't want to. I don't *want* to. I'll keep the room at the hotel—or book another."

The boat had gone, and in its place a tiny rowing barge crawled across the surface of the lake like a beetle on a pond. The sun had moved an inch in the sky.

I was holding her hand too tight and I let it slacken.

"Dwight and Andrews may not return till Thursday," I said.

"It's—ephemeral, all the other things one does not want of love—but it might last two whole days."

"If the angels are on our side," she said.

"I think they will be."

It was a rash and uncharacteristic statement of mine that events were going to bring in doubt.

CHAPTER 16

I left Garda at ten minutes to two and arrived in Verona with time to waste in the matter of changing stations. So I caught a tram outside the Porta San Giorgio and this took me along the river bank, across the Umberto Bridge as far as the Capitello. Then I took another tram from there.

In the Porta Vescovo there was no sign of Jane. I knew—as she did—that there were flaws in her scheme; but as the time came to act these loomed larger. To plan in theory is one thing.

I sat near the ticket barrier reading an account of Italian air successes in the *Popolo di Roma*. I thought I might have difficulty in recognizing Fräulein Leni Volkmann; but it was not so. A handsome young woman—but the sort you would instinctively describe as a young woman and not as a girl—five feet eight or more; no make-up of course; a gray tailored costume and royal blue scarf and gloves; pale skin, vivid auburn hair. She was wearing a "Napoli" armlet—"Napoli" being an abbreviation of the ponderous *Nazionalpolitischen-erzichungsanstalt.* It meant she was a teacher at an Adolf Hitler school. I wondered if she taught Good Behavior to the Young.

Jane arrived just before the train steamed in. She wore a halo hat and very short pleated skirt, which made her look innocent and almost in her teens. I watched Fräulein Volkmann get in a first-class compartment in the middle of the train. Jane walked toward the end to the second class. As the train was about to leave I swung aboard and began to move down the train, pushing past the people in the corridor. In the last coach Jane had found a place and there was one other seat vacant.

"Is this seat taken?" I asked an elderly man in the corner.

Jane did not look up, though it had not been arranged we should be in the same compartment.

"No. Someone has just got out."

I murmured my thanks and squeezed into the small space. There were three others on my side, two of them sailors. On the opposite side was the elderly man I had spoken to, Jane, a thin, nervous young man, and, in the window corner a good-looking woman of forty-odd who was just removing her hat to reveal shoe-black hair bound neatly with a close-tied veil.

The train chuffed into the first cutting.

From the start Jane began to prepare the ground. She dropped her glove and apologized to the gray-haired woman opposite her who stooped to pick it up. They had a brief conversation on wartime travel, and then there was a few minutes' pause while the effect of her foreign accent was allowed to sink in. Presently the dark woman asked if the other woman felt the draft from the window, and the woman deferred to Jane. Jane said no, no, not at all, and then apologized for her difficulty in pronouncing some words but she was, she said, an Americano. As conversation went on, she explained that her father was attached to a bank in Venice, and she had been at a finishing school in Switzerland and had joined him recently. She found the intonation difficult at times; it was awkward to know what you accented and what you did not. She had begun well and thought it easy, but really there was nothing easy about it. All the same she admired Italy and thought it the most marvelous country in the world and hoped she would never have to leave it.

The sentiment of the carriage warmed toward her. The elderly gentleman broke in with one or two comments, showing a tendency to veer around to the uncomfortable subject of the war and America's unfriendly attitude to the Axis powers; but Jane always steered him away from the contentious subject. She seemed to find just the right thing to say at the right moment and I, who am always short of small talk, marveled at it.

I did not join in, but now and then would lower my paper and stare at this slim, pretty, extrovert girl with the silk legs and the vivacious face and the ready wit, whom the sailors were now eying with so much appreciation, and wonder—not that the retiring, introspective, seemingly doom-dogged Robert Mencken should have fallen in love with her but that she should, *apparently*, have fallen in love with him. Life, I should know, does not work by probabilities: its prizes are distributed haphazardly.

The lady with the bound hair picked up a bag of grapes, but before eating them carefully drew on a pair of cotton gloves to avoid soiling her fingers.

We reached Brescia at two minutes after four. Here the thin nervous man left and another woman joined us. In wartime there was little likelihood of a compartment being too empty for Jane's plan, but the fuller it was the better.

The day was still brilliant, and the rays of the afternoon

sun struck across the carriage as the train gathered speed on the last eighty kilometers to Milan.

There were soldiers standing in the corridor now. I looked at Jane. She made no sign. Having done all that was necessary, she had fallen silent, and there was no conversation for some distance. The two sailors had taken ration cards out of their hats and were discussing them. They were on eight days' leave.

After some while the train slowed again and I had a moment's panic. But no, it was barely five o'clock. For the first time since leaving Verona I met Jane's glance, but there was no glint of recognition in it. Treviglio. The express surely did not normally stop here?

The lady with the hair-veil confirmed that this was a routine wartime stop and added that the train was running a few minutes late. Good news.

Off again. Due in Milan in twenty-five minutes—thirty if we were late. Testing time near. I wondered if everyone in the carriage could hear my heart thumping. The man next to me must, for you could see the beat of it in the tiny vibrations of my newspaper. I hurriedly folded the paper so that it should have no loose edges, tried to concentrate on the page.

No use. The Italians bitterly accused the Greeks of pro-British activities, of even allowing British submarines to refuel in their naval bases. This, the paper said, must stop— or it must be stopped. The fact did not interest me. I was waiting for a movement. I was waiting for a movement . . . I was waiting . . .

It came. The train had been steaming rapidly through the sunlit vineyards, the olive trees and the mulberry plantations for more than another ten minutes before Jane rose.

She put her magazine and gloves on her seat and turned to leave the compartment. Various people withdrew their legs to give her room to step past them, but in some manner—perhaps it was the swaying of the train—she caught her foot against the foot of one of the sailors and stumbled. She might have fallen against the open passage door, but put out her hands to save herself, and as she fell, in the most natural way in the world, one of her hands caught the handle working the communication cord. In Italian trains, as distinct from English trains, this is very accessible; it is suspended down on a polished chromium rod and is made in the form of a handle shaped to fit the hand.

. . . A curious whistling could be heard above the rumble of the train. Jane had saved herself from falling into the corridor, and instead sat for a moment in the lap of the elderly man by the door. Now she quickly recovered and stared up in horror at what she had done.

The whistling sound was lowering its note, became plaintive, ebbed breathily away as the train braked, died completely as it came to a standstill.

Silence. For a moment all was silence, as if the train and everyone in it held a breath. Then, growing in the place of the patterned beat of the wheels, a murmur of excited voices. At the same time seven of the eight people in the carriage began talking.

"Gee, I'm awfully sorry," said Jane, in English. "How ever did I do that?"

"Now indeed we shall be late," said the lady by the window, helping herself to another grape.

The soldiers in the corridor were the first outsiders to discover who was responsible for the mishap. When they had shouted the news both out of the windows and into the neighboring compartments, everyone, it seemed, wanted to peer into ours. Everyone began pointing out Jane to the people behind them. The people in our compartment took it rather well and explained carefully to each other just how it had happened. Jane went back to her seat and looked both timid and tearful.

"Whatever shall I do?" she appealed to everyone. "I never thought, you know. I guess I just put out my hand and never thought."

Everybody—excepting me—gave her advice. The lady next to her said, stay here and wait until someone comes. The elderly man on whom she had sat said, fear nothing, just explain to the guard exactly how it happened, just tell him the whole truth.

One of the sailors, who was now leaning out of the window, reported that there were six men on the line, no less than six officials. They were running backward and forward. Hooeee! This way! This was the carriage! Get out on the line and explain to them! said another woman.

"I don't know how it happened," Jane said, taking out her handkerchief. "I just trod on something and overbalanced—"

"The fault was partly mine," I said. "It was possibly my foot you stumbled on—"

"No, it was mine! It was mine!" claimed the other sailor, as if he was being robbed of some distinction.

By now there was a struggling and a heaving among the press of people in the corridor and two officials fought their way into view. Everybody was helping them and trying to explain to them just what had happened, and they apparently were trying not to listen. They forced their way into the carriage, one fat and pink and sweating, the other an elderly man who had been round checking the tickets. Behind them was a dark long-nosed man in a blue suit who bore the unmistakable expression of a Fascist official.

Some explaining had been done in the carriage by the time the third man got in. He interrupted it by shouting:

"*Now then!* Anyone who was not in the carriage when this happened—*outside at once!*"

His authoritative voice quelled the uproar. Two soldiers
and two other men were expelled, and he slid the glass door
in their faces and pulled up the window.

"*Now then!* Quickly. We have not all day to waste."

Four or five voices began but he cut them short. "*You,*"
he said, pointing to Jane, "if you are responsible—"

She explained it well. I had feared that before the inbred
suspicion of the O.V.R.A. her accident would sound contrived, but no one appeared to doubt its genuineness. The
man's sharp face twitched on hearing her nationality, and he
waved the ticket collector to examine all official papers in the
carriage. While this was being done, Jane dabbed her eyes and
continued to look helpless and sorry for herself.

The fat railway official said: "There is, you will understand,
signorina, a fine payable. You will see the warning on the roof
of the carriage. That must be met."

Jane looked uncomprehending for a moment, and then it
dawned on her and she opened her bag. "But of course. Of
course, I hadn't thought . . ."

The two railway officials looked pleased. A little money
would solve so much, would ease the whole situation. But
before Jane could pay, the O.V.R.A. man had turned sharply
on me, my passport in his hand.

"*You.* What is your business on this train?"

I stared at his angry eyes and realized somewhat late that
an American, whatever the attitude of the United States
government—short of war—would be treated with some
friendliness in Italy. A Yugoslav could expect no such treatment. There was Trieste and many other matters in dispute.

"I—travel in timber," I said, praying he would not ask my
name, which in the emergency of the moment I had suddenly, utterly forgotten. Brunsdorff, was it? Peter Brunsdorff?
Unglaublich . . .

"I did not ask what you traveled in—I asked what your business was on this train."

"I am going to Milan. I have a cousin living there. Dalla Marchetti, Via Valona, 22. I am leaving again tomorrow." All that came. But it was not Brunsdorff. It was . . .

"Did you come from Venice today?"

"No, from Garda."

"What business have you there?"

"I had often wished to spend a night by the lake. I broke my journey."

"When are you returning to Ljubljana?"

"Not for some days."

"Why not?"

"I have to go to Turin."

"What for?"

"To see the timber importers there," I said with a show of anger. "Your government wants oak wood. We have it to sell. It is a matter of common business!"

The man continued to stare at my passport as if hoping to see some irregularity. Jane was paying the two officials and tipping them. All annoyance had now been wiped from their faces as from a slate. Two guards had climbed up to the window from the line and were demanding how much longer. *No longer*, said the ticket collector. *Avanti!* It is nothing but a mischance. No damage. Right away!

As the train stammered into motion the O.V.R.A. man thrust my passport back at me. *Lansdorf!* God, what insanity to forget!

"You have been in Italy four days," said the man, "and you still have to conduct your business in Turin and Milan. What have you been doing in Venice?"

"I have to see the shippers," I answered patiently. "One was away. These things cannot be done in a few hours."

"You have hurt your hands," the Fascist said, looking at the bandages. "Was it in an air raid?"

There had only been a dozen bombs dropped near Venice since Italy entered the war, and he must have known it.

"It was a motor accident," I said, "before I left Yugoslavia. It is almost healed."

The man turned away and his eyes flickered toward Jane's bag. Jane fumbled in it. This, I knew, was a crucial moment. She could overtip the railway officials and they would think the better of her for it. But if she overtipped the Fascist it would rouse his suspicions afresh.

She took out a single note, but it was a good one. "I'm indeed sorry to have caused all this trouble," she said. "I hope you'll permit me . . ."

He took the note without looking at it and without thanking her. It disappeared, *flip, flip,* folded four times, into a top pocket of his waistcoat.

"Very well," he said. "Very well," and went out.

Jane sniffed into her handkerchief and then bravely put it away.

"Don't worry, child," said the woman with the grapes. "No harm has been done. And we shall still be in Milan nicely before dark."

I took out my watch. "We shall certainly be late," I said. "The time is five-thirty already."

The last half-hour was spent with a warm consciousness of success. We had asked at both stations whether the Milan-Basle express left promptly and were assured it did, even in wartime conditions. There was no question of this train being regarded as a connection for the other.

It would be unfortunate for Fräulein Volkmann. I wondered with what fuming impatience she had suffered the delay. No train can make up for a ten minute stop with only twenty-five kilometers to go—and anyway coal was too scarce to squander in the attempt. This was why Jane had left it so late. At last, relaxing, I began to feel I dared to look forward to the journey back to Garda. We could catch the seven o'clock train and be back in three hours. It scarcely bore thinking of. I could not bring myself to look at the girl opposite and to think of it. Yet I could not stop thinking of it. It was what I had thought in Garda this morning: live dangerously and all that matters is the next few hours. Perhaps to this is added: love dangerously and you have the world in your hands . . .

Straggling houses: we were running into the environs of the city: people were gathering up their belongings: train slowing. It was five minutes to six. We came slowly into the station.

People crowding now to get out; Jane ahead of me, and she was fending off one of the sailors who clearly thought he had been encouraged and wished to attach himself. I had no doubt of her ability to handle him. Of Fräulein Volkmann there was no sign. The whole arrangement had worked so perfectly that one could not help feeling anxious.

I pushed through the crowd and caught a porter by the arm. "The Basle express. I suppose it has left?"

He smiled briefly. "You are lucky, *signore*. You still have plenty of time to catch it."

"What!"

My voice must have been full of horror but he was too busy to notice.

"Platform eleven. There has been an accident on the line where the British bombed it. The express will not leave for twenty minutes yet."

CHAPTER 17

I met Jane outside the barrier. We went down the long flight of steps unspeaking.

"We must tell Andrews and Dwight," I said bitterly. "They will be somewhere on the train. I can buy a ticket and—"

"They're already in Switzerland," she said.

"In—"

"They're catching this train over the frontier."

I came to a stop.

"Walk on," she said. "We might be followed here. I didn't trust that Fascist on the train."

"Do you know their plan?"

"A little of it."

"And Fräulein Volkmann . . ."

"Will be a terrible complication."

"Is there any way of letting them know?"

"No."

I felt bitter and cold inside. All the false optimism and hope of the last half hour were blown away like dust which has accumulated in a corner. The success—the apparent success—had been too easy. One should never have trusted it.

"I must go, Jane. I have to catch the train. I know it means —the end of what we planned. But there is no other way."

She was lighting a cigarette. Her fingers were brown with nicotine. "Will it help? I doubt it."

"I might be able to help—at the time."

"Then I'll come with you."

"No. You mustn't be involved in what is going to happen."

"I already am."

"No . . . If we're—Jane: this is not for you—" I balked at putting it more plainly.

"And my passport's in order," she said, shaking out the match. "It was fixed before I left Venice, in case of accidents. Incidentally, is yours?"

We walked through the booking hall while I took out the passport. "Oh, dear God, no. The other one was. I was thinking of that . . ."

"Stop over here," she said, at a newspaper kiosk. We did so, and she turned the pages of a magazine. "I must go alone, Robert."

"Are you crazy? Perhaps I can get through without a visa."

"Not a chance. Did you say your other passport was in disorder?"

"Yes; you remember Andrews arranged it in Venice."

She looked at her wristwatch. "I might be able to get that. It will be in the Lorenzo store rooms if it hasn't been destroyed."

"What, get it now? You'd never manage it in the time! Besides, it might be dangerous, going there."

"Not to the store rooms. It's five minutes by taxi."

I hesitated. "There'll be traffic at this time . . ." While I half objected I knew I was going to agree, if she failed to get back in time, at least I would be sure she could not be implicated in what was to come.

Her hands tightened over her bag. "I'll do that. It's worth the chance . . . You, Robert, I think you shouldn't hang about the station, in case the O.V.R.A. man from the train is still around."

"I'll take a taxi too," I said, "just drive somewhere and then come back. I'll meet you at the barrier in fifteen minutes, No. 11."

"Get the tickets," she said, "and book to Lucerne."

I raised my hat with a formal bow as she left me. I had intended it to be an Italian bow, but in a moment of hypercriticism it suddenly seemed to me too Germanic.

After a few seconds I followed her to the entrance of the station and got in a taxi and gave the address that I had given the detective in the train. I had no idea in what part of the town this was, but when we had gone about a mile, having become certain that no one was following, I told the driver to return to the station.

He stared and shrugged but obeyed, and within ten minutes of leaving I was in the queue to book two second-class tickets to Lucerne.

Here I had a moment's leisure to wonder whether Andrews and Dwight would approve of our taking the train. It was impossible to decide whether our being there could help or hinder. There was still a tremendous impulse to opt out. But I could not feel there would be any true repose for either of us at Garda if we had not only failed in our mission but failed to warn them that we had.

I got the tickets and walked to the barrier nearest Platform 11. Standing close behind the ticket collector, reading a paper, was the hook-nosed Gestapo agent who had followed me all yesterday.

I drew back as if burned, cannoned into somebody, turned with a mumbled apology, strode quickly away. I did not think he had seen me.

I knew my face was white, as if I had seen a ghost. I had indeed seen one, the ghost of yesterday's fears. I had completely forgotten my minor changes of appearance. Would they deceive a keen and practiced eye?

But so far I did not think he had seen me. By the closest of margins, the margin of a lowered newspaper, I had drawn back in time.

How did I catch the train, then? There were other barriers. Would they admit me at another? Why was the man at No. 11? The merest chance? Jane must be warned. Where could I stand to warn her?

"How long before the Basle express goes?" I asked an official who was hurrying past.

"I cannot promise anything. If you're going you should take your seat."

I walked slowly into the great entrance hall. This place was conspicuous, but everyone entering the station must come this way.

Still no Jane.

A whistle, and I could hear a train move off. A secret and not quite respectable self hoped that it was the express. We had failed then but failed honorably. Andrews would have to cope with the extra difficulty of a woman on the scene. That was his job. That was his peculiar genius. Why sacrifice two days together in Garda and everything we had hoped for? Once again my mind dwelt on Garda as on an oasis of happiness and forgetful peace, a green and lovely thing offering me a woman's soft arms, in place of a murderous exploit which was not of my seeking and incalculable dangers I was not equipped to face.

No Jane. Supposing in our absence the Gestapo had told the O.V.R.A. about Lorenzo's and it had been raided. Supposing she had walked straight into a police trap.

People stared at me as they went past, and I knew my face must be betraying too much anxiety. After being pale it was now flushed. My cheeks burned. I forced myself to adopt a dull, noncommittal expression.

I saw her at last, paying off a taxi. She came running across the hall, threading her way between slower-moving people, almost dancing in her steps. I went across to meet her. She looked surprised.

"Has the train gone?"

"I don't know. I have not been able to tell." I turned with her and we hurried back through the booking hall to the next flight of steps.

"Why were you there?"

"One of the men who followed me yesterday—is watching the barrier—at platform eleven."

"One of the Gestapo? Have you been seen?"

"No, I think not."

We branched off at a tangent, reached another barrier at the extreme left of the station.

"Has the Basle express gone?" to the ticket collector.

"I don't know, *signore*. It may have. Platform eleven at the other end."

We passed through and broke into a run.

The German at the other barrier might or might not see us; I put a handkerchief to my nose. Fourteen, thirteen, twelve, eleven . . .

"There she goes," said a porter. "Just off now."

There were whistles as we ran down the platform. The train was moving.

"In here," I gasped.

We scrambled in breathlessly. Someone slammed the door behind us.

The last stage of the journey had begun.

CHAPTER 18

We found two seats in a second-class carriage near the front of the train.

In between boarding and finding the seat I had gratefully removed my spectacles, since as Edmondo Catania again I no longer wore them. We had traveled more than three quarters of the length of the long train and had seen nothing of Miss Volkmann or Dr. von Riehl. The first-class carriages were in the center, and there were several compartments marked "reserved," of which two already had their blinds drawn on the corridor side.

There were four other people in our compartment, so there was no opportunity for private conversation. After a while we went out into the corridor to admire the view.

I received my passport.

"Give me the other one," she said. "I'll keep it."

"No. There is danger for either of us in having two."

"I have an extra one for myself anyway."

"For yourself?"

"It was provided for me some months ago—in case of trouble. A different name etc. I guess it seemed a good thing to have on this trip."

"What did you hear at Lorenzo's?"

"Dwight and Andrews left soon after us. I was lucky to get the passports. Ricci and Dorio are burning everything that's unnecessary and burying the rest. Have you a cigarette? I'm clean out."

I lit one for her and gave her half a pack. She could hardly live without them. "You spoke as if you might know something of Andrew's plan. Are you sworn to secrecy?"

"No . . ." She inhaled gratefully. The draft in the corridor blew the smoke horizontally from the end of the cigarette. "It's really quite a simple plan."

"Andrews' plans usually are." I suspected he had suggested to her the idea of the communication cord.

She glanced up at me. "Oh, so you've noticed that."

She paused as we slowly entered a cutting. It was here that two carriages had been derailed. Gangs of men were busy in the twilight clearing the debris. It was some time before we were quite alone again.

"Beyond Lugano," she said, "you know the climb up to the San Gotthardo tunnel and the twisty descent at the other side . . . There are a number of little stations where even the expresses stop. At this time of year there are always climbers or skiers who want to take advantage of the first snow. They take the trains up to one of the higher stations, spend their day up there, and in the evening catch a train down again."

She tailed off as a man passed us.

"Yes?"

"Well . . . there are two extra skiers today."

"Oh," I said.

"They'll join the train at one station and leave it two or three stations later. Nobody will take any notice of them. Nobody will know—until later—what they've done."

I smiled grimly at the darkening landscape.

"And Fräulein Volkmann?"

"She's our responsibility still."

There was a long silence between us until Jane had finished her cigarette. "I'll see if I can locate them," she said. "Von Riehl might recognize you."

We reached Como just as it went dark. The night was a deep cloudy moonless dark, and the absence of lights in the countryside made it blanket-like and oppressive. On the train the corridor lights were dimmed and the blinds pulled in all the carriages.

I wondered if this delay in the train might upset Andews' plans as well as ours. Instead of the express reaching the Alps shortly before nightfall, the time would be about eight-thirty. Most of the skiers would have caught the earlier trains.

Jane returned to the compartment before we reached Chiasso. She nodded her success.

The gaunt frontier station was cold and drafty. We had already climbed from the Lombardy plain, and this was a first breath from the snows of Switzerland. The halt was a long one. Restrictions had recently been tightened up, and currency difficulties added to the delay. We all had to get out and stand in queues by the light of shaded blue lamps to have our money checked and our passports and visas scruti-nized and stamped. I did not notice von Riehl or his red-haired girl friend, so perhaps they were exempt from the formalities.

I took a chance and declared less money than I carried, since I still had a fair amount left and did not want to have it confiscated. The Swiss wanted to know my business in

Switzerland, and I said I was visiting my daughter who was at school there and that my stay would be only three days.

At last it was over and we climbed back into the train, grateful for the warmth of the carriages. Jane had only her thin summer coat and skirt. We were first back in our compartment and she said:

"They're going to have dinner shortly. I hope Vernon reckoned on that."

"It may be over by the time he gets on."

"I'm not sure. These train meals take a long time, and they haven't started yet."

I stared speculatively at the empty seats opposite. "Do you imagine that perhaps this might be our chance, this dinner they're having?"

"To deal with her?"

"Yes." One's mind balked at its own suggestion.

"Not unless we see Vernon and Dwight first. We can't move without their agreement. But what did you think of doing?"

I was prevented from replying by the return of the rest of the passengers. I was not sorry, for the idea was still too vague—and in any case it was too renegade an idea for me. Possibly Andrews' example was bearing fruit.

I decided to reconnoiter for myself. This was a train of twelve coaches, and I went from one end to the other.

Few people were standing in the semidarkness of the corridors, except in the third class. This darkness would work to our advantage.

Although electric, the train was making no apparent effort to catch up on its lost time. Two coaches behind ours was the dining car. Here, as one passed down the center of the coach, with the blinds drawn on either side, lights were much brighter. I avoided a waiter who wished to show me to a seat and another with a steaming bowl. Many were already dining, but not the two I sought.

Another carriage. Then the "firsts." The blinds of all were of course compulsorily drawn, but outside one marked RESERVED two men were standing. One was a reedy little man with eyeglasses and close-cropped hair, the other a tall powerful young man in the black and silver uniform of the *Schützstaffel*.

As I passed I rested my hand on the door handle of the engaged compartment for a measurable few seconds. At once the S.S. guard clicked his heels and said in a metallic voice:

"Ein reserviertes Coupe. Kann ich Ihnen Helfen?"

If I had not moved my hand he would have struck it away. *"Nein, danke schön,"* I said, and went on.

The prey was located. But in so strong a defensive position as to be almost invulnerable. My bowels twisted in fear.

So as not to arouse suspicion I stayed at the end of the train for some time before beginning the long return. The situation had not changed. I wondered what was going on behind the drawn blinds. Two people were there instead of the one that Dwight and Andrews expected. In view of the fact that —presumably—von Riehl's secretary had been sent to stand in the corridor with the S.S. man, were the doctor and his girl making love in the privacy of the compartment? *Kraft durch freude.* I would not have put it past them.

Lugano at last. Sitting quietly in the train, I began to slip the bandages from my hands in spite of Jane's reproving looks. Scabs were forming over the cuts; better with hands free. I also explored the bump on the back of my head. This was very sore still, but did not hurt at all unless touched.

Jane was chain-smoking and I think the woman next to her found it troublesome. It is odd, the blockages in the memory: I can remember every face on the Verona-Milan train, scarcely anyone who was in our compartment of the Milan-Basle express.

Jane finally got up and went out again. When she came back she made no sign but presently scribbled on the margin of a magazine that "they" were now at dinner but had only just begun.

At last we stopped at Bellinzona; and here the tension really began, for at any station now two skiers might join the train, and in the blackout it was almost impossible to see.

We took up a permanent stand in the corridor; here, at least, since we were in the front of the train, it was possible to scan each platform as we slowed to a stop.

Two stations whose names I could not see, and I began to lose a sense of distance. Somewhere, possibly at Chiasso, our engine had been changed for a more powerful one, and you could feel it pulling up the increasing gradients. Tunnels were becoming more frequent. We took wide curves on banked rails, the carriages tilting, doubling our tracks as we climbed in loops.

A third stop. Jane gripped my arm. Two men in heavy ski clothes, carrying sticks and skis. Then a clump of three men, then five.

"Careful," I said. "Are you certain?"

"It was the first two. The fat one. They'll get in at the end of the train."

"There's time," I said. "They can't move at once."

"We shall have to pass through the dining car to reach them," she said.

"Wait here," I said. "If I'm not back in fifteen minutes come through to meet me."

I opened the nearby door and climbed down the three steps to the platform. A whispered protest followed after me.

Colder than ever out of the train; the icy wind might have come straight from Golgotha. I began to walk as fast as pos-

sible down the platform: the guard whistled: I was opposite
the dining car when the train began to move. I sprinted down
to the next carriage, climbed the steps, pulled at the door
handle. It was locked.

I dropped off. Instead of running one way I had to run
the other. The guard shouted a warning. I jumped at the next
steps and clutched the rail: the unexpected acceleration of
the train wrenched at my sore hands. *"Lieber Gott!"* I said,
and turned the handle of the door. It opened and a friendly
hand helped me inside.

"Dangerous to cut it so fine, *monsieur,*" said a voice in
French. It was one of the skiers. I was glad it was not Andrews.

I thanked him, wiped stinging hands surreptitiously on a
handkerchief. Only a smear of blood came away.

I began to walk toward the rear of the train; but it was
hardly possible to open every carriage door; one just hoped
for the best.

Through two third-class carriages. Outside one were some
skis and ski boots. I pulled back the door, peered in, then
apologized and shut it again. Total strangers, all staring.

On again. In the next coach two men were standing in the
corridor talking. So this was it: Jane had been right.

I tapped a thick round back on the shoulder. "Excuse me,
there are seats in the middle of the train."

A big, bearded man turned and scowled. I thought I had
made an insane blunder but the other man muttered:
"Mencken!"

Both wore beards. How genuine these would have looked
in the daylight I do not know, but they were convincing in
the half dark.

"What in hell are you doing here?" Andrews muttered.

"Our contrivance failed," I said, "because this train was

thirty-five minutes late leaving Milan. The German woman is here. Also Jane."

Andrews' expression did not alter much, but I felt like a subaltern reporting some inexcusable failure to a commanding officer.

"What were you doing on the other train? I told you to stay in Garda."

I told him.

"So that's how you obey instructions . . ."

I explained briefly further. He of course was entirely in the right and I in the wrong.

"And now, why are you both on this train?"

"We had to warn you. And perhaps in some way—we can help."

"How can you help?"

"I don't know. Four are better than two."

"Who told you that? Whoever did was a fool."

I held my tongue and no one spoke for a while.

Andrews grunted. "Where are your glasses, man? You haven't a vestige of disguise!"

I told him I had had to become Edmondo Catania again.

"And what if you were followed? What if you were picked up again on Milan station?—"

"I was not. I saw them but they did not see me."

"This is no place for Jane Howard," Dwight muttered.

"I know that," I said angrily. "But I have no authority over her! We could only act as we thought best."

Two people passed us, and Andrews began to discuss the relative disadvantage of short skis. He used the Swiss-Italian dialect fluently. The train was steadily climbing.

"What is their position in the train?" Andrews asked grudgingly. "I presume you have discovered that." He struck a match and I glimpsed his profile, the short fleshy nose, the curved forehead under the navy-blue woolen cap. The profile was what one would chiefly recognize, even though the little plump cleft chin was hidden. . . . The match went out and the end of the cigar glowed.

"Jane is in the front coach. Von Riehl and the girl are in the sixth from the front, in a first-class compartment marked reserved. His secretary and an S.S. guard stand outside in the corridor. At the moment von Riehl and the girl are having dinner in the dining car, which is the fourth car from the front. They are as yet barely halfway through."

"It's what comes of the delay. But it may not be altogether a disadvantage."

"Jane will be coming through to join us soon. She'll be able to report on how quickly the meal is going."

"Stay here," Andrews said. "I want to see the first-class carriages for myself."

I put a hand on his arm. "Before you go, I have an idea— just an idea for the—for the temporary disposal of Fräulein Volkmann. I don't know if it will fit in with your other plan but—"

"What is it?"

We creaked to a stop before a little mountain station. Some people got out. We moved off again. I told them my idea.

Andrews said: "You're learning, Mencken. It's as good a makeshift as any. What station was that, Dwight?"

"Farola."

"In fifteen minutes we shall be in the St. Gotthard Tunnel. It all depends . . . Wait here."

He was gone, slipping away suddenly for all his bulk among the rumbles and shadows of the train.

We stood in silence staring out into the darkness. Sometimes fir trees could be seen, their branches reaching toward the windows, sometimes rocks part-covered with snow, a house, a rushing stream.

Dwight said nothing at all. Now it was nearing the point

of action I began to wonder whether I could go through with it. It was no longer the principle of the thing that I gagged at. This was a matter of heart and blood and stomach and the most primitive secretions.

I kept saying to myself: remember Dollfuss slowly bleeding to death on the Chancellery floor while the soldiers watched. Remember Calinescu and Roehm and a hundred others. Remember a hundred *thousand* others, packed in death trains for the concentration camps, bombed helplessly in their homes, machine-gunned as they struggled with their pitiful belongings on the roads of France. Remember your own father. This is total war. This man, this von Riehl, is as much an apostle of frightfulness as any of his breed. If this gas can be manufactured he will not hesitate to use it on London. I ought to be aghast at my own squeamishness.

I was, but I could not dispel it.

Dwight stirred beside me. "It's quite a while since I felt like this, old man. Real going-over-the-top feeling. You know. First light in the sky, just enough to see the hands of the old ticker. One minute; half a minute; *now!* . . ."

The sound of his voice was a help to me. Some community of feeling was established. We were closer together now in sympathy than we had ever been.

Dwight said: "D'you know, it's funny, when I was waiting to go over the top I always used to think about horses. Riding a chestnut mare across the Sussex downs, f'r instance. Feeling the air biting your cheeks, feeling the ripple of her muscles under your legs. Or comin' in to breakfast after a ride, sweating a bit and fairly glowing with the exercise, ready to eat a side of bacon . . ."

We went into another tunnel.

"Is this the St. Gotthard?"

"Doubt it . . . Or wiping the mare down, or hearing her whinny with pleasure when she heard your footsteps; the smell of the stables, the creak of harness. Or out across broken country—takin' a fence in your stride, giving her her head, easing her to make the best of a tricky hillside. . . . I always used to think of that sort of thing waiting for zero hour. Dunno why. Sort of escape, I suppose."

A railway official passed. The secret police, who traveled on almost every important train in Italy, had left at Chiasso.

Dwight sighed. "D'you know, old man, it's funny to think chaps like me will soon be unique. The first and the last trench war. There was only one and there'll never be another. Back to the war of movement again. A crying pity the cavalry have had to be mechanized—"

Andrews came back, big and ominous.

"I've seen Jane." To me, accusingly: "You hadn't told her your idea."

"I did not suppose you would approve it!"

"Well, I've told her. Act on it. Go along and make contact with her, Mencken: she's in the carriage between von Riehl's and the dining car. When they come through, there should be a fair chance. It's a toss-up, of course. . . . They should be out any minute now so there's no time to lose. As soon as you can, come along to us in von Riehl's carriage. We shall wait until you come before we act."

"Very well." I think my voice quavered in the middle.

"After it's over," Andrews said, "be ready to leave the train at the next station. That's all. And good luck."

I began a nightmare journey through five carriages to meet Jane. There were griping pains in my bowels as if I'd been struck with enteritis. My legs would hardly hold.

In the first-class carriage the S.S. guard still stood in the corridor. He was chewing something. The door of the compartment was a couple of inches open, and through the nick the little secretary could be seen with a typewriter on his knee. The compartment next door was also part open and was empty, and light flooded out. Now that we were in neutral territory the blackout precautions were not so stringent. I shut this door as I went past it and could fancy the Black Guard's suspicious stare.

As I entered the next carriage I came face to face with Dr. von Riehl.

Fortunate that the only time we had met in a good light was in the bedroom in which Professor Brayda lay dying and when he had had attention only for the man on the bed. Later in the hall the light had been poor.

He stared at me as if conscious of some latent recollection, then squeezed past. That high-colored, choleric face with the half-moon glasses, the tall broad-shouldered stoop, were very familiar to me, brought our task down to its rock-bottom reality. But at least he was alone. . . .

Jane was waiting halfway down the next coach. She was pulling on her gloves.

"Thank God you've come! I thought we'd be too late. It's madly difficult—so many people are coming back from the dining car."

"Remember, two raps," I got out, touched her hand, turned back, entered the lavatory at the end of the carriage, bolted the door.

She was right—we were only just in time. So now there was no more waiting.

The two raps on the door came after only a couple of minutes and I unbolted the door again, squeezing behind it. Jane came in and turned one of the taps on. Then she slipped out again, leaving the door half ajar.

"Do forgive me," I heard her say in halting German. "This hot-water tap will not stop running. Could you please help me to turn it?"

"What is it that you want?" came a strange woman's voice.

"This hot-water tap. See. It will not stop . . ."

The tall figure of Fräulein Volkmann came into the lavatory. With utter incredulity in my soul I put a hand over her mouth and my knee behind her knees, and pulled her back against the wall. . . .

In my romantic, sheltered life I had, I suppose, come to look on women as frailer, gentler creatures than men. This was my disillusioning.

Fräulein Volkmann reacted with the violence of a wrestler, thumping her head against my jaw, biting at my hand, jabbing with her elbows. I almost lost her.

Jane had squeezed in, bolted the door after her.

"Right pocket!" I snapped.

The German girl fought her mouth half free, gave a scream which was stifled as Jane thrust a glove in her mouth. In the tiny space there was no room. Volkmann twisted, pulling Jane with her, thrust her knees against the wall and kicked. At that moment in self-defense I forgot she was a woman, and hit her hard somewhere about the kidneys, at the same time throwing my whole weight on her so that she gave at the knees. My shins were scarified with her high heels. Twice I hit her again, while Jane dragged from my pockets the bandages that had been round my hands, and began to tie her ankles, then a rough gag with her gloves.

Somebody was sobbing for breath: it took time for me to realize I was making the noise myself. It was as if my civilized, logical brain was sobbing for something lost. A skin of reason shed.

I watched her and held her while Jane tied her hands and elbows and knees. She went on struggling, her green eyes like daggers while she fought.

"You go on," Jane said breathlessly. "I can do the rest."

"She may get free. She's—very strong."

"She won't! Hurry! Every second . . ."

I struggled upright painfully in the confined space. My hands were bleeding again, but this time where they had been bitten. Jane would have to stay here all the time. It was the only solution, for the lavatory door could not be locked from the outside. At least she would be out of what was to happen next.

I listened, carefully opened the door, slipped out. The door clicked behind me. There was no one near. A man was moving away up the corridor.

The train whistled and we rushed into the St. Gotthard Tunnel.

CHAPTER 19

There were two people in the first-class corridor. One was the S.S. guard, standing legs apart and hands in pockets, swaying with the train. The other, at the far end, was Andrews, bearded, in his ski clothes, a haversack still belted across his shoulders. The S.S. guard turned suspiciously as he saw me come into the corridor but was just too late to catch the nod I gave Andrews. I stared out of the window; a lantern now and then flashed past in the tunnel.

How long was the tunnel: ten minutes?

When I looked again Dwight was there too. They spoke to each other and Andrews laughed. They started moving down the corridor toward the Black Guard, Dwight some way behind Andrews.

The corridor was not wide, and as Andrews reached the German he excused himself and evidently made some joke about his bulk. The German did not smile but drew back against the door of the compartment, his hand on the pistol holster at his side. Then Andrews hit him, with a knuckle-duster, so quickly that I could not follow the blow. With one hand the S.S. man took out his revolver and with the other flung up an arm in a reflex action to fend off the blow that had already landed. He gave at the knees, blood spurting from his mouth.

Andrews caught him. As he did so Dwight slid past, thrust aside the door of the compartment and went in. There were two thuds, half smothered by the entombed rattle of the train, then quite distinctly the report of another revolver.

Andrews swung round and into the compartment. I was about to follow, intending to drag with me the body of the S.S. man slumped on the floor, when the door of the next compartment slid open and a middle-aged gray-bearded Swiss looked out.

"Was that—I thought I—" He stopped at sight of the unconscious man.

We stared at each other. He retreated into his compartment. I followed and was just in time to pull him out of reach of the communication cord. Losing all restraint and half blind with fear, I twisted at his collar until his face went purple, then relaxed the grip and felt in his pocket for something to gag him. He shouted, but I lifted my hands in such a manner that the cry died in his throat. In my memory now was the sound of a dry cracking noise—it might have been another pistol shot.

Someone was standing in the door. Andrews: a revolver with a silencer tube in his hand: perhaps that sort of expression was in my eyes too.

"Who is this man?"

"He heard the shot."

"Bring him next door. Wait. The S.S. man first."

I waited. In a minute he was back, sweat dewing round his nose and beard.

"Now!"

I half dragged the Swiss to his feet and thrust him out into the corridor. At sight of Andrews' revolver he had gone paper-white as if he was going to faint.

I should have feared what I would see in the next compartment but now I had no ordinary feelings left.

The S.S. guard was lying bunched up on one seat. Sitting almost across his feet was the little secretary, glasses broken, a bleeding purple bruise on one cheek. Opposite him and covering him with a revolver sat Dwight.

The big off-side window was right down, and cold air was rushing in like a vacuum from the screaming darkness outside. There was no sign of Dr. von Riehl. His hat lay trodden under the seat, and on the seat were his wallet, his pocket book, some papers, a dispatch case. A smear of blood streaked the cushion of the seat; there was a wet stain on the floor. But Dr. von Riehl had gone. He was *gone*.

Dwight's mouth was twitching and twitching.

"Shut the door behind you," said Andrews, "and help me off with this!" In German he added: "I'll kill the first one who moves!"

I shut the door and helped him with his knapsack. Inside were fine strong cord, ready-made gags, little wedges.

These he used at once, slipping them under the door so that it could not be opened from outside. Then he snatched up the cord and began to bind the three prisoners. He seemed to put an extra viciousness into tying up the secretary, so that the meek little man flinched with every pull. While they were being trussed up, Dwight was going through von Riehl's wallet, pocket book and dispatch case, sifting through the contents of each, tearing documents and papers into tiny pieces and letting them fly out of the window. The revolver lay on the seat beside him.

When two had been bound and gagged Andrews said: "Now. Tell Jane and bring the woman here."

"We need your help for that," I said. "Or Dwight's. We need lookouts."

He paused and stared at me. "I'll come. Found anything, Dwight?"

"Yes," said Dwight. I could see him struggling not to cough.

We tied up the Black Guard. The man was still bleeding from the mouth, and I think his jaw was broken. It is difficult gagging a man in that condition but we had to do it, hoping he would not suffocate.

Andrews looked at his watch. "Four minutes of the tunnel left. Come on. We *must* leave at the next station: it'll be in about eight minutes."

We moved the wedges and left the compartment, went down the corridor, squeezed back to allow a couple of well-dressed ladies to pass, keeping our eyes down. I went ahead and came to the next carriage and the lavatory door behind which Jane and Fräulein Volkmann were hidden.

A man was waiting outside.

I stopped in utter dismay. It was an effort to keep my breath even, the muscles of my face still. The man glanced at me, went on with his cigarette. Andrews squeezed past us both, stopped a couple of yards away looking out of the window, leaving it to me.

I swallowed a lump of something and said to the stranger in German: "I hope you will pardon me, but I think you will find a lavatory vacant in the next carriage."

He took the cigarette from his mouth and stared again, a fussy, well-dressed man.

"Oh? But I have been waiting here several minutes." He spoke Swiss-German and clearly thought I was trying to cheat him of his turn.

"I'm indeed sorry." I tried to smile, but only my lips

turned, like a smile on a death-mask. "You see . . . it is my wife who is inside. She is a very poor traveler and suffers from train sickness. She may be there half an hour."

"Oh." He was still noncommittal, but after looking me up and down again he evidently thought I was not the sort of man to stoop to deception over so small a matter. "In that case . . . thank you . . . I will take your advice."

"Thank *you*," I said, with a rush of gratitude.

He drew at his cigarette and leaned against the window rail in a friendly way.

"My mother," he said, "was always a very bad traveler. Sea, rail or even carriage—any movement would upset her. It was a great disadvantage until, quite late in life, she went to a specialist in Zürich. He advised her to wear a belt."

We came out of the St. Gotthard Tunnel. The wild country-side showed up under the first glimmer of the rising moon.

"The specialist said—and I pass it on to you, *mein Herr*, for what it is worth—he said that ninety per cent of all travel sickness is due to insufficient support of the stomach and diaphragm. Any slight disturbance of the equilibrium, in susceptible persons . . ."

I looked at Andrews, who was looking at his watch. He had overestimated the length of time we had left. And there was a smear of blood drying on his sleeve.

"On application of the belt . . . you get the support that is lacking. It binds the stomach and diaphragm. My mother . . ."

"I'm afraid," I said, "I must ask you—"

He moved a step, then came back. "My mother, I know, recommended this treatment in at least five different cases, and in only one do I know of a definite failure. And in that case . . ."

"I must go and see my wife," I interrupted, and tapped twice on the door. "I . . . know you will excuse me."

"Of course. Naturally. I can see you are worried. But do not forget to recommend this expedient to her. Urge her to try it, for I assure you—"

There was a click as the door was unbolted.

"Sometimes it takes effect immediately; sometimes—"

"Thank you. I'll remember."

"And you will be saved the needless worry—"

I squeezed into the lavatory and bolted the door again. In here nothing had changed. The German girl was still on her knees, the gag in her mouth. She looked up sharply when I came in. Jane was standing behind the door. The sweat was dripping off my forehead on to my hands.

"Well?"

I nodded, not trusting my voice.

"Has everything—happened as it should?"

I nodded again. "But there is a man outside. I couldn't get rid of him. He may not have gone yet." I was taking deep breaths, trying to control myself.

The train went into another tunnel. You could feel the carriage banking to the sweeping curve. Some of these tunnels made a complete spiral in the rock. I forced myself to wait half a minute. Urgency had left a taste like cold copper in my mouth.

"Now," I said to Jane.

I unbolted the door and slipped out. Thank God the man had gone. Andrews had not moved. But coming down the corridor toward him was a Swiss railway official.

I wondered if he was examining tickets . . .

He squeezed past Andrews and as he did so said something. Andrews courteously replied.

He passed me. "Please to remember that blackout regulations are still in force."

"Thank you," I said.

Was he going into all the carriages? As he went on through

the connecting door and down the first-class corridor I waited for a shout of discovery.

None came. I went after him and peered down the first-class corridor. He had passed on and the corridor was empty. I came back and gestured to Andrews, who nodded back. I pushed open the lavatory door.

"Now," I said. "Take her legs. I'll take her shoulders."

In the cramped space it was horribly difficult to lift a dead weight. Then as soon as we got Fräulein Volkmann upright she began to jerk and struggle like a corpse suddenly galvanized with electric shocks.

Jane grabbed her feet and we tried to get her out. The German woman hooked her elbows round the door so that the door swung with us and jammed us half out. I kicked the door with my foot, but she twisted herself to hang on to it. She was rubbing her face against the wall to get her gag away.

"Quickly!" said Andrews behind me.

The train was beginning to slow down.

Andrews grabbed the woman's legs and tugged, and we came out through the door with a jerk that must almost have dislocated her shoulder.

We had to navigate past two closed compartments whose occupants I had not seen. We did this somehow. At the third, which had been occupied by the Swiss gentleman, Fräulein Volkmann bent her knees suddenly and kicked with her bound feet at the glass. A second kick would have shattered it, but Andrews hit her—only once—and she suddenly went limp.

We were almost in the station.

Andrews slid back the door of the reserved compartment and we struggled in. Dwight still sat with his revolver on the seat beside him, methodically destroying the last of the papers. Somehow he had got some fresh blood on his hand.

The three prisoners were where we had left them, except that the S.S. guard was recovering consciousness and groaning.

Andrews jumped across the carriage and thrust up the window; the blind fell back into place as we came to a stop.

I wedged the corridor door from the inside. "Well? . . ."

There was a brief silence as if we were all trying separately to estimate our chances of getting off here. The S.S. guard recovering, the woman not too securely tied. . . .

"Too late," said Andrews. "We've got to wait till the next."

"Go on, old boy," Dwight said. "You can manage it. I'll attend to the filly."

"Don't talk foolish," said Andrews. "Have you finished the papers?"

Fräulein Volkmann was stirring again. He had hit her somewhere on the neck.

After all the noise the station was strangely silent. The air was rarefied, quiet. Dwight wiped the back of his hand across his mouth and beard, and when it came away there was more blood on it.

"Go on!" said Dwight. "Don't be a cow. Next one may be too late."

"Jane," said Andrews, "tie up that woman, or she'll make trouble."

Jane went instantly to his rucksack and took out fresh cord. Her own hair was over her face as if she had been out in a gale.

"Mencken," said Andrews, and gestured.

I went at once to Dwight. "You have been wounded?"

Dwight sneered. "Get *out*, you fool, while the going's good! This luck won't last much longer."

"Where are you hit?"

"In the back if it satisfies you. Where else would that little

200

runt of a secretary shoot you? I didn't reckon he would be carrying a gun . . ."

The secretary cringed back against the seat, shortsighted eyes staring. Andrews had gone to help Jane with Volkmann. As she recovered, the German girl's eyes went round the carriage, looking for someone who was not there, and for a second her eyes met mine. I do not know if she guessed what had happened, but they were cold with hate.

I pulled Dwight's coat off, and dragged up his blue polo sweater and shirt, both of which were stained but not sodden.

The train began to move.

"Well?" said Andrews.

I pursed my lips.

"Go on, don't you know the difference between a doctor of chemistry and a doctor of medicine?" Dwight jeered at his friend. "I can tell you—without his advice. I've wasted my damned money on a return ticket."

Andrews looked at me. I shrugged. I thought most of the bleeding was internal. Yet if there had been much loss of color in his face, the sunburn and the beard concealed it.

"Could do with a drop of brandy," Dwight said to me.

"No, it's the worst thing."

"The worst thing's happened, old man. Be your age."

I looked at Andrews, who shrugged.

Dwight said: "You ought to have bloody got out then. False heroics—in this game. Lot of ninnies. Good God— thought you'd more sense, Andrews!"

The bullet looked as if it had gone into the left lung just under the shoulder blade. It had probably lodged in one of the ribs in the front of the cage.

"That haversack," Dwight said. "Take it or—destroy it. Nothing else here matters. Anyway, it's been a good gallop."

"What about von Riehl's papers?" Andrews asked.

Dwight shifted and wiped his mouth again with the back of his hand. "All gone. Gone with the wind. Confetti-size pieces. Thought it better—in case we didn't get away with them."

Andrews said to me: "Give him the brandy."

Jane handed me a flask and I passed it to Dwight who only just got it to his lips.

Andrews said to me: "How long d'you think?"

I shook my head. "I don't know."

"Your job's done, Dr. Mencken."

I stared round the vibrating carriage, at the four captive figures, and at the empty belongings of the man who was no longer there. Every time, I seemed to meet Fräulein Volkmann's hate-ridden, accusing eyes.

"And yours," I said to Andrews.

"Mine is never done. What passport are you carrying?"

"Both."

I was about to add more, but he glanced warningly at the three Germans. These were the witnesses to our deed. These two men and a woman—not to mention the innocent Swiss—would spread our description and what we had done all over Europe. If we had only been sufficiently ruthless to destroy them all our chances of escape would be enormously greater.

The same idea must have been in Andrews' mind for some time. He was watching me with a cynical, bitter glint in his eyes.

"This is the sort of job that strips the frills off you, Mencken. You might make a serviceman yet."

"No thank you." I had the very unpleasant feeling that he was already casting about in his mind for a successor to Dwight.

"Listen," he said. "Next station I'm going to get Dwight off if it's humanly possible. He's still just strong enough to walk and there may be a chance if he gets to a doctor. You and Jane will leave first and keep your distance. You don't know us—under no circumstances do you know us—understand?"

I said: "You can't manage him alone. I'll stay with you, and Jane can go ahead."

Dwight jeered. "You see what happens, Andrews, when the boss gets lily-livered. You're both fools! Save your own skins!"

For once his eyes were easy to read. Behind his bitter tongue his mind was calm, and clearer than ours, and he meant exactly what he said.

"Mencken," Andrews said, "and you, Jane; these are orders. Obey them. Go out into the corridor and move to the end of the carriage. When the train stops *get out*—I don't know the name of the station, but I'll get out with Dwight too. From there on we'll play it as it comes."

We were in another of the endless tunnels, rattling and swaying. I looked at Jane and she pushed back her hair and half-smiled back. Then she lifted her shoulders just perceptibly and bent to take the wedge from the door. I followed her out. The door slid to behind us.

She was fumbling for a cigarette; her face looked paper-colored in the subdued light; when she got the cigarette out she could hardly hold it between her fingers. I lit it for her. For a moment our faces were together, and I brushed my cheek against hers. Again she half-smiled, and she put her hand over mine.

"Low tide," she said.

I nodded. "This journey seems to have taken half a lifetime."

She said: "It's taken all of Dwight's."

I could see Dwight collapsing on the platform, railway officials running, the police called. If Andrews got him out alone he was doomed too.

"Ah, so, we have met again," said a voice behind me.

I swung round. It was the little man who had been waiting outside the lavatory. I stared at him nonplused, unable to think.

"Ah, so this is your wife." He beamed and bowed, holding on to the rail. "*Gnädige frau*, I am delighted. Yes, I must say she does not look at all well."

"She is better," I said stiffly.

"Of course stuffy carriages and cabins are the worst possible places. And smoking, I would have thought, no help . . ."

Jane tapped the ash off her cigarette and looked at me for a lead.

"Not many minutes ago, *gnädige frau*, I was talking to your husband on the problem of travel sickness. Possibly he has told you?"

"No," said Jane.

I groaned and tried to turn my back on him.

"Oh, well, I was telling him of my mother, who was greatly troubled and at length consulted a specialist in Zürich . . ."

He went on and on. I peered with sickly anxiety out at the countryside, now glimmering in long-shadowed moonlight. I doubted if Dwight would even make the station barrier. If, just possibly, we could get him as far as a hotel. But once he moved . . .

". . . all connected with the question of balance."

"Yes," said Jane. "Yes."

Was that the pull of the brakes? God, yes! Now was the testing time. If this fool did not leave us I felt inclined to knock him on the head and put him with the others.

"You will excuse me," I said. "This is where we get out. So we will wish you good night, sir."

We went over a bridge and heard the rush of water before we could see the hastening stream. A few houses showed, and a glimmer of light in one of them. The overhead trolley ran among a clutch of wires, and the tiny station we were entering was lit by a blue electric flash. What hope here? What prospect of competent medical aid?

The train came to a stop.

"A very lovely district for a holiday," the man was saying to Jane. "But—"

"Good *night*," I said.

I grabbed Jane's arm and we squeezed past him and climbed out of the train. I do not know if he wondered at our lack of luggage.

The change in temperature from Milan was drastic. This was midwinter. I put my arm round the girl and we moved in the semidark away from the circle of a shaded lamp, stood in a doorway and waited.

Only one other person had climbed down from the whole long train. We were almost opposite the exit. If Andrews and Dwight came now, at least there would be only a few steps to walk.

They did not come.

Jane was shivering.

A porter swung a storm lantern. After the noise of the train the night again seemed unnervingly still; we could hear a single conversation going on along the platform. The station was dark and steamy, with a fine wet mist hanging in the air around the dismal blue lamps. In the distance you could hear the whispered sibilants of a waterfall.

They did not come.

There was a whistle. The train was going to start again. Vile indecision.

"*Nur zu!*" I said.

She seemed by the movement of her body to be obeying almost before I spoke. As the train moved we clambered hurriedly aboard again.

CHAPTER 20

We stared breathlessly down that corridor I had come to hate more than any corridor I had ever seen before. There was a woman in it now, at the farther end: she had come out of one of the other compartments and was leaning on the rail looking out of the window.

"Stay here," I said. "I'll find out what's wrong."

"Why, I thought you were alighting here." It was the thrice-accursed bore again, his pink face shining. "Did I misunderstand you?"

"We mistook the station." I pushed roughly past him, nerves going now. Jane, keeping her head, stayed to talk with the man; her pleasant voice in its broken German followed me until it was drowned by the rattle of the train.

As I stood outside the reserved compartment a sudden frightening thought came to me that the two men had perhaps got off the train at the other side, that they would not be looking for us and we would still be on the train.

As I hesitated the compartment door opened and Andrews lurched out. For a moment he did not seem to see me.

"So it could not be managed?" I said.

He continued to stare out of the window. "Blast you! I told you to get off the blasted train!"

"We did, and waited for you to follow. Can you not move him?"

"No need," said Andrews. "Dwight is dead."

Still one more tunnel. So that was the end of the adventure for one of us. Von Riehl and now Dwight. An eye for an eye. Sound Old Testament philosophy.

I suddenly began to feel terribly tired. Even capture seemed better than this prolonged, never-ending tension. Odd that all Dwight's problems were solved. No need for him to worry about getting out of the country; he had given all his pursuers the slip. How strange one could get out of it that way. His body went jogging on but they could do nothing about it. It was not keeping to the rules somehow.

A waiter came down the corridor precariously carrying a tray of coffee. He squeezed past, went on past that self-important little fool who was prattling to Jane.

Andrews coughed and grunted. "I shall miss Dwight."

As we came out of the tunnel rain spattered on the window. Andrews took a swig of brandy from the flask and then handed it to me. In the better light he looked disheveled, suddenly rather adrift, as if for a surprising moment he had lost purpose and decision.

"We're in a hell of a mess," he said. "No good blinking that. Particularly you two. I can get along, but that German bitch will remember every detail of you two. She'd be better put out of the way like her master. . . ."

At last Jane had succeeded in getting rid of the man. I went down the corridor.

"Drink this."

She took a short gulp of the brandy. "What went wrong?"

"Dwight is dead."

"Oh . . ."

"Drink it all. There's little enough there."

She made a face at the second gulp and shuddered. "Oh, God, what do we do now?"

"Out at the next station, I suppose. It's a question of luck. . . ."

The lady who had been standing at the other end of the corridor now came past us. She looked at us disdainfully as if she suspected—rightly—that we had no business in the first class.

We listened to the beat of the train. The countryside was lightening every minute, even though the moon was obscured by cloud. Three compartments down, Andrews' bulky figure blocked the way.

Jane stirred against me. "Have you a cigarette?"

"Not now. Here it is. You can feel . . ."

You could feel the pull of the brakes. Andrews turned sharply into the compartment behind him, and the train was almost in the station by the time he came out with Dwight's haversack. He put a wedge under the outside of the door. In the dark it would be difficult to see.

More houses about a station somewhat larger than the last. Sidings, a signal box, some electric driving coaches. More lights.

Andrews beckoned us as the train stopped. "Not yet. In here."

We followed him into the empty compartment which the Swiss gentleman had unwillingly vacated. He slid the door. We stood about. Two or three people getting on and off.

"Sit down," Andrews said.

"You're cutting it fine."

"We're not getting off here."

209

"*What?* . . ."

"I've been working it out. The next station is Lucerne. We shall be there in twenty minutes."

Jane looked at me helplessly and then stared at Andrews. It crossed my mind that Dwight's death, which had obviously hit him harder than one would have expected, had brought on him this sudden collapse into weakness and indecision. Whether one should try to take control . . .

"A place like this," said Andrews. "A junction and a few dozen houses. We should have to leave the town and we might have difficulty in hiring a car. If we leave at Lucerne the chances are no one will remember us in a crowd. And once in Lucerne I know of places."

The train was still in the station, tempting us to disobedience.

But Jane did not move, and so I did not. This freak decision of Andrews, though perhaps at base the logical one, had every natural impulse against it. And sometimes natural impulses are best. If we calculatingly rejected this last bolthole in favor of a better one twenty minutes ahead, what might happen in twenty minutes? . . .

The train began to move.

"I'm backing my judgment in this." Andrews took off his beret and glowered at himself thoughtfully in the mirror over the center seat. "It's unlikely any official will want to come in these compartments before we reach Lucerne. And unless I'm forced to I'm not going in next door again either."

"You're not—"

"The train stops fifteen minutes in Lucerne." He began painfully to pull out tufts of his beard. "They may be discovered then or later. In either case the first question will be: who has done this? The second will be: where did they leave the train? If all the captives say: the last station before

Lucerne, it will divert pursuit and give us an extra chance. See?"

I saw well enough. But it was a gambler's throw.

"They will be left free to struggle for twenty minutes," I said.

"It's taking a chance on the knots." Almost all his beard was off now. "Let the window down."

I did this, and he screwed the crisp black hair into a ball and dropped it out. I caught a view of the broadening stream, swift-moving, oil-green and yellow in spate, twisting among the boulders on its ever noisier way to join the stillness of the lake.

I sat beside Jane, knees giving way from weariness and nervous exhaustion. Her hand when I found it was very cold.

"Have my coat."

"No . . . it's not that . . ."

Andrews said: "When we do leave the train we move fast. You're traveling on a false passport, Jane?"

"Hilda Fenburgh."

"Good. The question is how quickly you can get back to Venice."

I said: "You cannot possibly send her back! This is asking for trouble."

He stared at me. "I can see the dangers as well as you. The chief one is this Volkmann woman. But if Jane can return to Venice undetected she has her usual alibi there, and there should be no reason to link her with this case. Every foreigner in Italy can't be paraded in front of Volkmann. Had you those gloves on all the time?"

"Yes," she said.

"That's a help. I wiped everything in the carriage—"

I said: "It won't be enough! Fräulein Volkmann has been with Jane for a quarter of an hour: she will remember everything, what perfume she uses, the size of her shoes, the shape of her fingernails—"

Jane laid a hand on my arm. I knew then that, in spite of everything that had happened since, the decisions of Garda still held. It was a bitter knowledge.

"You can't, of course, take a train straight back," Andrews said to her. "The hunt will be up too soon. But I think I can fix something for you. It will depend. The first thing is for us all to go to earth in Lucerne. You needn't think, Mencken, that I shall run her into more danger than can be helped. She's only useful to us so long as she's free."

I did not say anything at all.

"As for you." He pushed his beret into the haversack, took out a crumpled trilby hat. "Your job's done and the sooner you're out of this the better. Your best course may be to make for Yugoslavia—via Innsbruck and Klagenfurt— though I don't suppose you'll relish passing through German territory."

I should not. The prospect filled me with extreme foreboding. "D'you mean we have to separate soon?"

"The minute we're out of Lucerne station."

"Oh, but surely—"

"And I want you to memorize these addresses. First you, Jane. . . ."

I peered under the blind again and saw we were now running near the lake. The water was in the shadow of the precipices on the farther shore and looked like a great black chasm in which nothing lived or stirred.

"And you, Mencken, to this address. Whoever answers the door you must say you come from Cousin Peter in St. Gall . . . Fortunately we have many friends in Switzerland."

Footsteps down the corridor. We all waited and listened. They came, passed, died. What was happening next door?

Supposing one of them managed to stand on the seat, get some sort of hold of the communication handle.

"I wish," Jane said, "I wish none of this had had to happen this way. . . ."

Andrews grunted. "Well, I'm sorry about Dwight. He'll be hard to replace. Here, Mencken, put this rucksack on."

I got into it with difficulty, for Dwight had been a narrower built man; Andrews began to adjust the straps.

"You never liked him, did you?" he said.

"Who? Dwight? Oh, that's not so." It had been Andrews I had not liked, but I could hardly say so.

"Probably not your type, Mencken. He was the sahib type . . . Not that his career had ever been very distinguished. He got turned out of Sandhurst for some shady business and went into the last war in the ranks. He only rose to be acting-major when the others were killed off. What difference does it make? He was a serviceman you could rely on for anything. He came to Italy in the first place because of his lungs. Did all sorts of poor jobs before he drifted into this. . . ."

The train was fairly racing now. Andrews dabbed his face with cream, and then wiped it.

"Some people thought him a snob. Maybe you did. Maybe snobbery is different in Vienna. Dwight hated soiling his hands . . . And mad crazy about horses, even though he'd never owned one since his Sandhurst days. I think he took this work not so much because he liked it as because it helped him to live nearly the way he wanted to. Hungarian with a bit of money. Flat in Rome. Enough to eat and drink and smoke. But it was no good asking him to do the dirty work. He'd got to be the gentleman. Oh, well. But for *this* piece of dirty work tonight he *insisted* on taking the chief part. . . ."

I peered out again. The lake had now come full into view, glimmering like a silver dish in the moonlight.

"Your ticket," I said sharply to Andrews. "Did you not book only to one of the mountain stations?"

He nodded. "But I helped myself to one of the through tickets to Basle. They'll pass me out on that."

The brakes were on.

"Good-by, Mencken," said Andrews. "I'm not coming through the barrier with you. You and Jane can risk it together if you feel like it."

He had a soft greasy hand.

We were in the suburbs of the town. Sweat was on my forehead again and I brushed it away. I had never known a train take so long to stop.

At last signals, another train, lights, points, we came into the station. And stopped. The platform was on the corridor side. Jane rose, but Andrews held up his hand. There were footsteps and we waited for them to pass. Voices on the platform, the usual bustle, the usual shouts.

Andrews got up.

At that moment, from the compartment next to ours, a woman began to scream.

CHAPTER 21

"Fräulein Volkmann," said Andrews, "has got rid of her gag."

These were the last words I heard him speak as he led the way toward the door of the carriage.

Our wait after the train had stopped had cleared the corridor, and there was no one about. So far no one, it seemed, had heard the screaming. We reached the door and were blocked going down the steps by a porter lifting down baggage.

"Porter, monsieur?"

"No," said Andrews.

"Porter, mad'moiselle?"

Jane shook her head.

I was last out, and as I got down I thought I heard someone going down the train toward the screaming. It was almost inaudible from outside the train because of all the other noises. There were not enough people about to hide us. And the lights were too bright.

On the long walk to the barrier Andrews stopped to buy a paper. It meant that we should reach the barrier well ahead of him. It was a generous gesture and one for which I shall always hold that unlikable man in special esteem; for it was a race against time; the moment the contents of the carriage were discovered the barrier would be closed.

A small queue of people were waiting to pass out. We fell into line. A man at the front of the queue had stopped and was arguing because he was being asked to pay extra.

I turned and stared down the platform for the expected running official. None yet came. Andrews had joined the queue about fifteen people behind us.

We moved up, came to the ticket collector, handed over our tickets and were through. . . .

We walked slowly out of the station. Jane leaned against me, and I think she was feeling faint. Near the very entrance I steered her into a dark shadow.

"Are you . . . ?"

"No, I'm O.K."

"I think we must wait and see if Andrews is clear."

We waited.

Through a break in the clouds the moon came out, flattened at one side like a lemon that had been trodden on. The town roofs glistened with drying rain.

Andrews did not come.

"I must go back and see," I said.

Her grip tightened on my arm. "There may be another exit . . ."

Then Andrews came. We saw him at the back of three or four others, walking with a slouch, his hands in his pockets. We let him go by, knowing his anger if he had found us waiting. Then we followed.

But soon Jane stopped. "This isn't your way, Robert. We'll —have to separate."

"I *must* see you safely to your place."

She shook her head emphatically. "In a few minutes the whole town will be out. They'll telephone Goldarthe and find no one of our description left the train there. Then they'll comb Lucerne. The Swiss police are efficient. We've perhaps ten minutes at the most."

I hesitated, haunted by my own sense of futility and doom.

"Not for long," she said, "it may not be for long."

"How can we know? The odds are so much against us."

"Odds are often that way."

"While you are still in Italy . . ."

"It may not be for long," she said, like a child trying to comfort herself as well as me.

We were in the deep shadow of a house when we said good-by. I remember the keen but no longer cold freshness of the air after the musty heat of the carriage; I remember the brightness of the moon on the other side of the street and the darkness of our shadow as if we were under an awning; I remember the distant whistling of a train.

I remember Jane.

"Take great care," I said.

"Take great care," she said.

I kissed her eyes and found them wet. I buried my face against her neck and took a deep breath, trying to remember by touch and smell and heart, trying to remember.

Then we broke apart and went our ways, she in the direction of the lake, I toward the river and the old town.

Never have I felt so much alone.

I slept that night in a gaunt old house above the Mühlen-brücke, slept heavily despite everything, and for fourteen hours. It was the last undisturbed sleep I was to have for some time.

Most of the next night I lay hidden among milk cans in a van jolting westward.

Westward not eastward, I was relieved to note. Although I had hardly been consulted in the matter, I was aware that an organization was coming into operation on my behalf and no pains were being spared. Before daybreak we reached Lausanne, and there I went to earth for seven days while the hue and cry must have raged about me. (For murder is murder and is a civil crime of the first degree, and war did not, could not, enter into it. And it did not matter who had fired the shot, we were all equally culpable. And it had happened on Swiss territory, and it was of paramount importance that the Swiss government should not give Hitler any cause to take offense.)

The man who sheltered me was head of a big dried-milk business, and although on the one occasion I met him he was prosaic and rather unfriendly, he did his job well and fed me well and hid me well, and that was all that mattered.

During those seven days of waiting there was nothing to do but try fretfully to rest, and worry over Jane, and in the night be disturbed by constant tangled dreams in which the train usually figured. But sometimes I was outside the door of Lorenzo & Co. hammering on it while the Gestapo crept up behind. And sometimes I was back in Vienna after my father's arrest, listening for the tramp of studded boots.

Always I would wake sweating and sit up and peer round the loft, trying by a recognition of semi-familiar things to find reassurance. But the incubus of fear sat on my shoulders and often would not move until the coming of first light.

It was an actual relief when the time of waiting was over, and in spite of everything the rest had done me good. My head had quite healed and only throbbed occasionally when I bent down. During this interval my hair was dyed black, and I was encouraged to shave lightly each day with a very blunt safety razor so that by the end of the week there was a strong dirty stubble on my face.

On the Friday night I left Ouchy in the back of an old peasant's cart and we jogged along to a hamlet west of Vevey, where I boarded a small boat taking market produce down the lake to Geneva. In the gentle evening breeze the vessel was allowed unaccountably to drift near the south side of the lake, and here one of the two brothers manning the boat rowed me ashore in the dinghy—very grudgingly, for it had been contracted that I should swim, and this I had never learned to do—and very gingerly, with scarcely moving oars, although previously he had assured me that there were never guards nowadays at this point.

I slipped over the side into three feet of water and waded ashore.

In the cloudy dark it was difficult either to see or be seen, but I found the railway embankment I'd been told of, crossed the line, and moved silently on into France. There was no alarm.

It could be that the worst was over. Within certain limits I was now a free agent. I carried French papers and had a plausible story if challenged; though I meant if possible not to be challenged. I was dressed in an old walking suit with a knapsack in which, among other things, were French currency, a brandy flask, a small bottle of hair dye marked *Lung Tonic*, a torch, a map, a pocket compass.

Unfortunately, though I speak German and English and Italian almost without accent, my French is not good: there is always for some reason a guttural undertone, and although the words come freely I am not above grammatical mistakes or groping for the right expression.

Almost all the way to begin I followed that railway line—

since the Haute Savoie is no country to wander in indiscriminately even with the help of a compass. Traveling by night I made a detour to avoid Evian and Thonon, and spent the next day, a wet gray autumnal one, under a haystack south of Lully. The next night I came again within measurable distance of Swiss territory and was glad to change course and strike south, first because where there are land frontiers the lonely stranger is always suspect, and second and more important because I was not far from German-occupied France, and the last thing I wanted was to blunder into some pocket of territory which my map did not show.

I lost my way four times. The whole district was on the verge of mountainous, and to avoid worse mistakes, I followed the valley of the Arve. Off my route by ten miles, I slept that day near St. Pierre, but moved on again by the afternoon, feeling progress was too slow.

Annecy at long last, reached and skirted. Fatigued and footsore I was tempted to stop early, but went on and shortly after struck the main Lyons road. Here there was good luck: an old lorry stopped and a hoarse voice offered a lift. Knowing I ought to refuse, I climbed gratefully in and was in Lyons by ten in the morning.

Having had my story and my indifferent French accepted without question by the gray-haired driver of the lorry, himself from the Loire, I began to feel more comfortable about both. I caught the afternoon train for Marseilles.

From a room in a cheap lodging house off the Place de la Joliette I began to frequent the rambling dock area of the largest city of unoccupied France. Not for me the handsome offices of the *Compagnie Générale Transatlantique*. Just someone who, for a consideration, might accept a passenger or sign me on as a member of the crew and ask no questions. As a last resort I had been given an address to use but advised to shift for myself if possible.

On the second evening, conversation with the master of a tramp steamer who had put in that morning and was leaving on the Monday for Rabat with a cargo of bricks and tiles. He would call at Barcelona and Tangier. He said yes, he would not be averse to taking a passenger if one came along with the money, though the accommodation was poor and no comfort to speak of. Why anyone should wish to travel with him . . . He looked sidelong at me.

"Were you wanting to leave the country in haste?"

"In a way," I agreed. "Mind, there is nothing wrong, but I have no exit permit and I hear it takes weeks sometimes to get one through. And here's my uncle in Tangier offering me a good job if I can get there next week."

The seaman sipped his drink. "You will not get out without a permit," he said somberly. "They have tightened up everything since I was here last. Orders of the Boche, they say. The docks are watched day and night."

"Why is that?"

He shrugged. "Plenty of people the Boche wants are still in this corner of France."

"But why co-operate to help your enemy?"

"The German is no longer the enemy, my friend. He is the victor. There has been a treaty signed, you remember."

"I should be willing to pay well," I said. "I would have thought an arrangement could be made."

"With me, ah yes. With a sensible man, money speaks. But not to the danger of his own business." He considered me regretfully, shook his head and sighed. "I would do it of course if it were not certain to fail. Too many already have been caught. If you have nothing to hide, monsieur, get your permit and we will talk business."

Two other conversations followed this general line; the second man openly suspected me of being a German agent sent to try to catch him out. It meant that I must ask for help after all.

At the upper end of the Rue Noailles is the Restaurant Anglais—an ostentatious name, I felt. M. Gaston, the proprietor, although he had been notified of my possible arrival, was not at all anxious to help, but he agreed that an attempt to leave the country without proper authority was ill-advised—if the proper authority could be got. To be caught boarding a ship without correct papers would be the end of me. He looked me up and down, not disguising very well his opinion that if he had to risk his own freedom he preferred to do so for some distinguished combatant unmistakably French, rather than for a polyglot of some sort with a bad record. However, grudgingly he agreed he might do what he could; his brother-in-law was a *juge d'instruction*. If I would leave my *carte d'identité* and passport with him and call back on Saturday night. . . .

"How safe am I without papers in the meantime?" I asked.

"Not safe at all. Do not go out. Come about this time on Saturday."

As I left he added: "There are many German agents in Marseilles, and in some cases they are attempting to supervise our own police arrangements. It is necessary for everyone to act with the utmost caution."

The next three days I spent indoors, but ordered newspapers and read them with apprehension. Though no account was accurate, the best and fullest was in a paper published on the previous Sunday when I was struggling out of the valley of the Arve.

"From our Zürich Correspondent.

"Further dramatic light has now been shed on the murder of Dr. von Riehl, the highly placed German official, in the Milan-Basle express of last Wednesday week. The crime is now attributed to the activities of a famous British spy and saboteur who recently arrived in Italy and is directing wide-spread attempts to disrupt the Italian war economy.

"In a fracas which developed while the train was passing through the mountainous San Gotthardo region, one of the assassins who had been hired to commit the crime was also killed. He is thought to have been a Hungarian of the Magyar aristocracy. The other has so far escaped all efforts to bring him to justice.

"It is known that the British agent was himself on the train at the time and took a part in the crime. This has been established by a member of the German delegation who was trussed up with bandages which had been used by a Milanese hospital the day before when the secret agent was treated for minor injuries following a street accident.

"There has been an acceleration of the pursuit, and an arrest is expected shortly.

"A British official interviewed in Zürich last night declined to comment on this report. If the truth is as stated it would appear that the European war is about to enter on a new and bitter stage, not unlike the internecine terrorism which for some years preceded the outbreak of war last September."

It was disconcerting to think of the bandages. On what else had we slipped up? It was disconcerting also to be invested with the major part. The angle from which the article was written disturbed me. Dwight had seen further than Andrews in the matter. How far would we be regarded as common criminals elsewhere?

On Saturday by the midday post a package was delivered addressed to me. Inside were my papers returned: stamped on a page of the passport was my exit permit. An unsigned note said: "Do not call here again. Do not relax your precautions. Avoid the police."

It was more than I had dared to hope. From experience

coming out, I knew that I should have little difficulty in getting a Spanish transit visa once I reached Barcelona. That night I found the French skipper who was leaving on the morning tide on Monday for Barcelona, Tangier and Rabat. He agreed to take me.

CHAPTER 22

The first wan light of Monday's daybreak was barely showing over the harbor as I walked through the drizzle to
the Bassin Lazaret. The tramp steamer *Grive*, was easy to
find in the semidarkness; she had had the French colors
newly painted on her superstructure, and three men in greasy
overalls were retracing the flag painted, for the better view
of airmen of all nations, on her hatch.

The dock was empty. A seagull screamed its welcome to
the dawn. With a sensation of release I turned to go up the
gangway. A hand touched my arm.

Two men, one in civilian clothes, one a policeman.

"Monsieur is a passenger in this ship?"

"Yes."

"Please to show me your *carte d'identité* and exit permit."
It was the civilian speaking.

I handed him what he wanted and he scrutinized them
with a torch and then scrutinized me. The policeman flashed

a torch in my face. The papers were returned. "You will kindly come with us."

I looked my alarm. "What?"

"You must come with us."

"For what reason?"

"We wish to ask you a few questions."

"Are my papers not in order?"

"New instructions have been issued that all persons leaving the port shall be questioned by the police. A special watch is kept for those who try to slip away in cargo boats."

I thought for a moment of some desperate bid to escape. My eyes ran the length of the ship. One man had splashed the first stroke of blue paint on the hatch. The captain was not to be seen.

"Your authority?"

"I am the authority," said the policeman.

I shrugged dully. I felt overwhelmed by this ultimate defeat on the very brink of freedom. "Very well."

I did not enjoy the walk to the *préfecture*. "Avoid the police," Gaston had written. In any event, if I were arrested, my real identity might be established, and that would be the end.

In the *préfecture* I waited half an hour in a bare white-washed room and then was taken into another room where there was a *Commissaire de Police*. He was a tall dark man with a long narrow nose and a soiled collar with untidy flapping points. At another desk under the window sat a uniformed policeman who looked very sleepy but occasionally roused himself to take notes.

The plainclothes *agent* explained in a few words and then left, but the policeman who had been with him took up a position by the door as if, absurdly enough, I might try to escape.

The *Commissaire* fixed me with a very sharp gaze and then

began to thumb through my papers. I knew that the stamp imprint covering the passport photograph had been faked, and it was possible that the exit permit also was a forgery. I felt that this was not a man who would miss much.

"Julius Favel," he said at length.

"Yes, monsieur."

"Kindly explain your reasons for leaving France."

I did so. I had been working in Morocco for some years prior to the war. At the outbreak of war I had been ill, but in May of this year had come to France to join my regiment. Because of the collapse of France I had not succeeded in doing this in time, and after staying with relatives in Lyons I had decided to return to North Africa, where an uncle, who lived in Rabat, had offered me work.

The story sounded thin and unconvincing told in this gaunt, lofty room under the piercing eye of the *Commissaire*. I began to see it would never do.

Silence except for the sound of the thin man opposite breathing through his nose.

"You speak French indifferently for a Frenchman, M. Favel."

"I was born in Saigon."

"So I see. Your father and mother were French?"

"They were French nationals. My father came from Bordeaux but my mother was Annamese."

The *Commissaire* rolled himself a cigarette.

I said: "My father died young. I was brought up by my mother so that French has always been my second language."

"You have lived long in France?"

"No, I have never lived in France; I have only been on visits."

He blew a few specks of tobacco off the desk. He sniffed as if conscious of an artificial smell about the story.

"Your papers seem in order. When was this exit permit issued?"

My tongue stumbled. "Last week. I think you will see the date on it."

"Present times are exceptional, M. Favel. Those who book passages in unimportant cargo vessels and attempt to board them at dawn for a noon sailing are apt to arouse special suspicions—at a time when every traveler is suspect."

"I see that now. I am sorry."

He began to cross-examine me about my work in Tangier and Casablanca before the war, about my movements during these recent weeks, about my uncle who offered me work in Rabat. I groped in my imagination for many of the answers and hoped they sounded more convincing to him than they did to me.

"Ah, well." The *Commissaire* yawned and rubbed a hand distastefully over the stubble on his chin. "That is the way of it. We are at sixes and sevens in this country just now." He shoveled the papers together and thrust them at me. "I think you may catch your ship."

I could have wept with relief. "I shall be most grateful. Thank you."

He blew smoke past his cigarette, and flecks of white ash floated over the desk.

"Thank you," I said again, putting the papers in my pocket.

"The police of this city," he said, "are grossly overtaxed. All these extra duties. Watching the docks and the shipping offices. Keeping a check on the many aliens and refugees. At present we are looking specially for a criminal with newly healed scars on his hands, who it is thought may have come this way. He is wanted for the murder of a Nazi official in Switzerland. That sort of thing."

I stood there as if all my blood had gone.

"Oh," I said.

"Yes," said the *Commissaire*. "Before you go, monsieur, please to show me your palms."

I knew then that this was the end. I knew that he had seen through my story all the time and had been toying with my excuses for his own amusement. Forgetting the bandages had been the pitfall. This was an identification before which ordinary disguise fell away as useless.

Stiffly I took a step forward and extended my hands, palms upward. It might have been much better if the chase had ended at Lucerne station and saved all the rest. Let M. *le Commissaire* get what credit and pleasure he could from the capture. I could only—

"Thank you, monsieur. That is all. Maurice will show you the way out."

At the sound of his name the sleepy policeman at the other desk rose and surreptitiously stretched.

I stared at the *Commissaire*. He had looked at my hands and now was dusting away fresh cigarette ash which had fallen like snow on his desk. His expression had not changed. I looked quickly at my hands: in the electric light the scars were plain to be seen.

"Do you," I began. "I—"

"I, too, am an overworked man. Regulations and precautions. New instructions from this source and that." He shrugged and his eyes blinked at mine through the smoke. "But one carries on. One tries to obey. And at the same time one tries to do one's duty as one sees it."

I struggled to speak. "Perhaps you will—"

He got up. "Show this gentleman out, Maurice. Good day to you, M. Favel."

I went out, walking with a distinct effort, not yet quite able to realize why I was free, not able to thank as I should have wished a man who contrived to serve France in her downfall but did not forget old friendships or old friends.

CHAPTER 23

I reached England in early December. We put into Liverpool one evening about six; although it was damp I spent the last hours on deck watching for signs of the land which had shown up some time ago but now had disappeared again with the fall of night. The cold salt air filled my lungs.

Arriving back was not quite so inconspicuous as departure had been. On the dock was Colonel Brown, limping and gray-eyed, to meet me.

I shook hands, surprised and slightly flattered that he was here. He peered at me in the indifferent light.

"Good to see you back, Doctor. You're looking tired. With reason, I expect."

"I am a bad sailor," I said, "and we have been at sea sixteen days."

He smiled. "You'll spend the night with me? Then you can go home for a rest—without any fear of internment."

"Is my sister well?"

"Yes. But we could not notify her in time of your arrival. Also I wanted a private talk with you first."

We drove to his hotel for dinner. It was, for wartime, a good dinner, but I was too concerned with other things to be able to savor it.

He had had two reports, but naturally wanted me to fill them in. He was polite enough to wait until dinner was over. Then I told him the whole uneven story.

"Dwight," I ended, "in the carriage Dwight destroyed everything he could lay his hands on. There would be nothing of value, I am convinced, found on von Riehl's body when it was recovered. So, unless something unexpected of Professor Brayda's was found, the record of his researches is likely to die with the two men."

"Except for what you know."

I shrugged. "If you will arrange me a meeting with Carruthers or Dyson or someone of their standing I will explain what I know, but it is hardly likely to be enough to work on. Even supposing you thought it desirable to work on it . . ."

Colonel Brown did not speak.

I said: "But I think I must warn you that scientific discoveries seldom occur in a vacuum. Sometimes there is one pioneer, but more usually it is as if the climate has become ripe for this or that discovery, and a man in Japan will be only a few months before or behind another man in Paris or London. At this moment there may be someone else somewhere in the world who is thinking along the lines of Professor Brayda."

He frowned, his quiet introspective frown. "It is a risk we have to take."

"Yes, it is a risk we have to take."

Silence fell.

He said: "This has not been a pleasant experience for you,

232

Dr. Mencken. It turned out all so very different from the way we expected things to go. I'm afraid you'll get no official thanks."

"I did not expect it."

"No . . . J.41 may even get a nominal reprimand. It is not the way we want to wage war."

All this time I had been urgently wanting to ask him questions. "Am I to take it that reports have come direct from—"

"From J.41? Yes. He is back in Italy. Naturally I know no details. K.9 is also back."

"K.9?"

"The woman agent you came in contact with."

I moved muscles gone suddenly stiff. K.9. To me only was she a woman, living and breathing, with fine skin and dark eyes and soft hair. To Colonel Brown she was K.9. It was strange that not until the very end of the adventure had I come so close to the conventionals of the trade.

"As for Captain Bonini," said Brown. "If he is of any further use he will be used. In this work we can't afford to discard a traitor just because he is a traitor to both sides."

"She is safe?" I said. "Where is she; still in Venice?"

His eyes met mine in surprise. "The woman? Yes, she is still in Venice."

"I would think it dangerous for her to be there."

"As a matter of fact," he said, "if you are interested, there is no harm in your knowing that J.41's second report, just received, requests permission for K.9's recall."

"I am certainly interested! And greatly relieved." Then with new alarm: "For what reason?"

"In Milan a part of our organization connected with a dress shop has been raided. Fortunately we were well forewarned. But there is the risk that through the shop some connection may be traced with K.9."

"Dear God, yes! She is leaving?"

"I have sent instructions," said Colonel Brown dryly.

"And how long will the instructions take to reach her or Andrews?"

"About a week."

"In the meantime?"

"In the meantime they will use their own discretion."

I tried to see it reasonably. "The German police—"

"The Gestapo are flooding northern Italy. They are always the advance guard. If the Italians fail to organize their own war machine the Germans will take it over. There will be no backing out or making a separate peace."

"I know the Gestapo too well," I said. "Their efficiency. Their ruthlessness. If Mrs. Howard leaves it one day too late . . ."

"The German police have their limitations. They slipped up badly over you, didn't they? I think it would be a mistake to worry unduly. J.41 is not above acting on his own initiative. Indeed, his one failing is that he does this too much."

I said: "J.41 . . . Andrews . . . may have the one failing you speak of, but he seems so much at home in his work; really, one would guess, he seems to enjoy it. One is curious, against one's better judgment, about his background."

"I have not studied his dossier and could not give you the information if I had it. All I can tell you is that his name is not Andrews, that he was born in Swansea, the only son of a prosperous clergyman."

"Of a . . ."

"Yes. I understand he led a sheltered life. His father bought him a junior partnership in a firm of architects and he went out to Italy to study. He never came back."

"Oh," I said.

"His father and mother are still alive. His father is Suffragan Bishop of—well, of a Welsh diocese. Their son has been a great disappointment to them."

Through the gray smoke of the colonel's cigar I seemed to see curling the ranker smoke of one of Andrews' interminable green cheroots. I tried to imagine him deep in theological discussion with a shadowy, white-haired figure in gaiters. My mind would not face the picture.

I spent that night at the hotel, the best in the city. Half its bedrooms were uninhabitable; my window was boarded up.

I was back. I was home. Colonel Brown had expressed his government's gratitude for services rendered and had said that my naturalization papers would be through in a matter of days. Then I would be English officially, in fact, however much my deeper impulses remained polyglot.

There was now no longer any need to concern myself with Andrews. I could forget Bonini and poor Dwight and the rest. I could put away the perplexities of human nature and return to the more predictable reactions of the laboratory. By tomorrow evening I could be back at work.

The thought did not thrill me, as three months ago it would have done. If fifteen years of study and research had quite unfitted me for the dangers of secret service work, fifteen weeks as a secret agent had left me curiously, psychologically unfit for a return to the laboratory. At least to begin, I felt I should have no patience for it, no concentration, no singleness of mind. Almost, an invitation from Colonel Brown to take on some other task would have seemed, perversely, more inviting.

I had suffered a sea change. I would never be the same again. Introspection had been invaded by action. Mental tubes, previously clogged with the overrational processes of civilized living, had been blown clear. This certainly had not made me a better man, but it had made me better suited, and perhaps more reconciled, to the age in which I lived.

I turned and tossed through half the night, thinking of Jane. The news that she was to leave Italy filled me half with elation and half with dread. Andrews would not have been prepared to dispense with her unless he was convinced of her danger. There were days of waiting ahead now, perhaps weeks, before I heard anything at all. Equally well I might learn of her capture and probable death or of her freedom and another chance.

"I am not a quitter," she had said. "After the war, Robert . . ."

But after the war was too long.

It would be a strange alliance if it ever came, someone like her, so much of the new world, with someone like me, so much of the old. The extrovert and the introvert, the attraction of opposites. A sudden enormously strong physical attraction which in a few meetings had quickly become something more.

But it hardly occurred to me that it might not work. We complemented each other; we did not clash. Her first marriage might be a warning that she could change: I did not care. It might on my part be the confidence of ignorance; what was it on hers?

I had come out of this traumatic adventure sure of very little; it was good to be sure of one thing, and it was good not to have to base that sureness on logic.

I only wished I could have been as confident that we should get the chance to try. How much was she implicated in Lorenzo & Co.? How quickly would the secret police move?

Toward morning I went to sleep and woke about eight feeling, without good reason, more rested in mind. Mornings are not usually an optimistic time; perhaps this was some illusion of confidence induced by the slits of sunshine falling, this cold December morning, through a crack in the boards across the window. Only time would show.

There was a dark winter still ahead. But I felt we should see the spring.